Readers love *New Leaf* by ANDREW GREY

"For the majority, the story is like going for a walk in your favorite park… a pleasant excursion allowing for reflection and figuring out a way forward with life."

—Love Bytes

"If you like ex-police officers, ex-actors, hurt/comfort, with a touch of mystery and suspense and some mild man-sex you will love this one."

—TTC Books and More

"Andrew Grey does such a fantastic job of creating characters that are real and genuine and he's done it again with *New Leaf*! They are not perfect people, but real people going through real things and they give me all the real feels!"

—The Geekery Book Review

By Andrew Grey

Published by Dreamspinner Press
www.dreamspinnerpress.com

By ANDREW GREY (CONT)

Published by DREAMSPINNER PRESS
www.dreamspinnerpress.com

By Andrew Grey (cont)

Published by Dreamspinner Press
www.dreamspinnerpress.com

IN THE
WEEDS
ANDREW GREY

Published by
DREAMSPINNER PRESS

5032 Capital Circle SW, Suite 2, PMB# 279,
Tallahassee, FL 32305-7886 USA
www.dreamspinnerpress.com

This is a work of fiction. Names, characters, places, and incidents either
are the product of author imagination or are used fictitiously, and any
resemblance to actual persons, living or dead, business establishments,
events, or locales is entirely coincidental.

In the Weeds
© 2022 Andrew Grey

Cover Art
© 2022 L.C. Chase
http://www.lcchase.com
Cover content is for illustrative purposes only and any person depicted
on the cover is a model.

Mass Market Paperback ISBN: 978-1-64108-269-3
Trade Paperback ISBN: 978-1-64108-268-6
Digital ISBN: 978-1-64108-267-9
Mass Market Paperback published November 2022
v. 1.0

Printed in the United States of America

To Dominic, who always has my back. And for Mary Lou—she's gone now, but she still inspired the story.

CHAPTER 1

VINCENT ROBINS stood on the sidewalk in front of the late-Victorian house he'd grown up in, its brick exterior, white moldings, and gingerbread porch trim achingly familiar. A peeling shutter hung at an angle above the porch, where one of the hinges had given away. The once-impeccable lady was a shadow of her former self. His mother had always kept the house beautiful, with paint touchups each year and the porch swept every day. The yard and gardens had been tended and full of color, not the way they were now, weed-infested and almost frightening-looking, like they belonged to a witch from a children's book. Vin sighed and lifted his suitcase, carried it up the front porch, then used his key to let himself inside.

At least the interior didn't show the same neglect. The furniture he remembered was all in place, if a little more worn than the last time Vin had been home.

"Dad?" Vin called. He wandered into the small kitchen that his mother had redone a few years before she died, and then on to the family room. Footsteps from the floor above alerted him to his father's whereabouts, and he turned back the way he'd come.

"You made it," his father said flatly. He always knew how to roll out the welcome wagon.

"Yes. My plane was on time and everything." Though it had been draining as all hell. The flight from Los Angeles had been fine, if long. But when you added the drive up from Baltimore, the entire journey went from tiring to exhausting. "I can see the place needs some work."

His father humphed. "I called the guy your mother used for painting. He retired. I had a contract with another painter; he retired. I have someone coming next week… unless he decides to throw in the towel and file for Social Security too." He actually smiled, and Vin was relieved to see some part of his father still there, inside the shell of residual grief he had worn like an overcoat ever since his wife's passing. Mack Robins had always been the life of the party, quick with a joke and a smile. He could keep a room of their friends spellbound for hours. But now the light was gone and so was the humor. It was as if his wife's death had snuffed out the best part of him.

"That's good, Dad," Vin said with a smile of his own. The two of them had never been particularly huggy, so their smiles were as close to a warm greeting as they got.

Vin hefted his bag up the steep stairs to the room he'd grown up in. It had been redone some time ago but was comfortable enough, and he set about putting things away and getting settled for his visit.

The bed sure looked inviting, and he dropped down on the edge of the mattress with a yawn. His legs ached from being stuck in a plane for nearly six hours. He was hungry and he needed sleep badly.

"I'm making some lunch!" his dad called up the stairs.

"Thanks. I'll be right down." He really didn't want to move, but he forced his body to do it anyway. In the tiny kitchen, he offered to help, but there was never room for more than one person, so he wandered into the living room and looked out the large windows. "I take it you didn't have any luck selling the business."

Robins Flowers had been a staple business of Carlisle, Pennsylvania, for decades. Now that he was approaching seventy and without his wife, Vin's dad hadn't had the heart to keep it going. He'd closed the business right after she died. He'd hoped to sell it, but that obviously hadn't happened, and now the shop and attached greenhouse sat alone on the other side of the road behind the house, looking sad and forgotten. The glass greenhouse panes were dirty but seemed intact. Still, the shop was shuttered and lifeless, which Vin knew would have broken his mother's heart.

"Not really. Your mother and I made a go of it all those years because everyone knew we were here. But it wouldn't be the same for anyone else. The place is off the beaten path, so whoever took over would have to spend a lot on advertising. So far people just haven't been all that interested." He popped some bread into the toaster. "There was one couple I thought might buy it, but they practically wanted me to give it to them, and I wasn't going to do that. I could sell just the land for more than they wanted to pay. So now it sits, your mother's and my life's work, just rotting away."

"You could have kept it going," Vin protested.

His dad shook his head. "Not without her. Your mother was the one who loved the business, not me. She was the one who talked the customers into huge bouquets of roses and designed all the displays and arrangements everyone wanted. I didn't do any of that. When your mother died, the heart of that business went with her. I didn't have anyone who could take over what she did." For a second Vin thought there might have been a dig at him somewhere in that. "You were off living your life, and… this place, the town, the house, none of it seems the same without her. I can't tell you how many times I have wished that I could just die and get it over with."

The toast popped, and he put down another set before getting some ham and turkey cold cuts from the refrigerator. Judging by what Vin saw inside, his dad ate a lot of sandwiches and warmed-up store-bought soup. Not that Vin could blame him—cooking for a single person was never a lot of fun. Variety suffered, and making a large amount of anything meant you ate it until you never wanted to see the stuff again.

His dad made his sandwich, and Vin then took his turn and got drinks before they sat in the family room to eat in front of the television, where his dad had a ballgame on. "I didn't know you liked baseball."

"I don't," his dad said. "But I gotta watch something. If you want my opinion, I hate watching television, but there's nothing else to do. Your mother and I used to love working in the shop. It was what we did. You remember. The two of us were never apart, not in almost forty years of marriage. And now I'm alone." He ate and turned his attention to the game. "Getting old sucks."

"Yeah? Then do something about it. Dad, you're sitting here watching a sport you don't like. Do you have any friends you could go out with? What do you do?" He was concerned that his dad was just moldering away.

"You have no idea what it's like here." There was no venom in his dad's voice, just resignation. Heck, Vin would have felt better if his dad argued or told him to go to hell. When he was a teenager, they had fought regularly about anything and everything. But back then his dad had passion and opinions. Now he watched television programs he didn't care about just for something to do. His dad used to have fire, spunk. Now he had sandwiches in front of the television on a TV tray.

Vin didn't argue, simply ate his lunch and drank his glass of water. His dad seemed content, and once Vin had some food in his belly, fatigue caught up with him. He took care of his dishes and went upstairs to lie down. After he kicked off his shoes and pulled the light blanket over himself, sleep came easily.

The ballgame was over by the time he returned downstairs and found his dad asleep in his chair. The house was quiet, and with nothing to do, Vin pulled open the sliding glass door and wandered out into a backyard that was in need of mowing. He could do that tomorrow—it would give him something to do.

He looked around, taking in the old, red-painted garage, and then his gaze settled on the old flower shop once again. Vin was thinking about wandering back there to take a look around when someone emerged from around the corner of the shop. That was odd. But then he remembered there was an old trail that ran from the middle school through the woods behind there. Still, he decided to take a closer look.

Vin hoped that someone hadn't tried to get into the shop to see what was inside. With a sigh, he wandered over to it. No windows were broken, and the door was locked when he tried it. Vin peered through the window. Everything looked the way it always had: the old counter, stands that once held some of his mother's creations pushed to the side. Dust covered everything. He kept walking, checking out the back of the building. If someone had gotten inside, he didn't know how. The shop looked closed up tight, and Vin turned to check out the greenhouse.

It was a shame that his dad hadn't been able to keep the place going, but Dad didn't have Mom's creativity. She had taught Vin everything he knew, though, and it was because of her that he had a job in one of the premier floral houses in Los Angeles, whose client list included stars of the stage and screen. Vin had designed arrangements for Oscar winners and royal baby showers. No job was too big or too small, and Vin's talents were always in demand. The only reason he'd been able to take time off for a vacation was because he'd gotten ahead on his design work for while he was away.

He wandered around to the front of the greenhouse. Its windows were as dirty as the flower shop's. Vin shook his head. It was such a shame. Maybe the business could have remained viable if his father had hired a floral designer. But the simple thing was that his dad's enthusiasm for the business had ended once Mom died. And Vin realized he would have to be the one to do something about it.

For one thing, the buildings were starting to look derelict and uncared for. No one was going to buy something in this state of disrepair. If his dad was going to have any chance at selling, the place needed to be cleaned up, the weeds and scrub that had sprouted cut away, and the lawns mowed. Even though the business was no longer running, the place had to look like someone cared about it.

And that job was going to fall to him. Heck, it looked like a lot of things around here were going to end up in his lap.

Well, what had he really expected? His dad had worked hard all his life. Maybe he deserved a rest. But it would have been easier for Vin to deal with if his father hadn't let everything go to shit.

"Vin," his dad said as he came out to join him. "What were you doing?"

"I thought I saw someone out there," he said without turning to look at him. "Dad… while I'm here, I'm going to do some cleaning up around the shop. I'd also like to meet with the agent who's handling the sale for you. Could you call them?" It made his heart ache to know that selling meant letting part of his mother go. But it had to be done.

"You don't need to," he groused with a sigh, as if looking up a phone number was more work than he could bear.

"Why? Do you want it to just fall down?" Vin snapped. Then he wished he hadn't. He took a deep breath. "If you're going to sell, then we have to make it look like it's worth buying. So I'll try to clean it up, and the agent can come and take fresh pictures. Maybe we'll get some new people interested if the shop doesn't look like something time forgot."

"It's just too much work, and I don't have the energy," his dad said.

Vin turned to him, seeing his eyes filled with sadness and longing. Now Vin understood his dad's reticence to go inside the shop. Being there reminded him too much of his mother, and his father still missed her like a limb. He got that. But letting the place fall into ruin wasn't doing anything to honor her and the work she'd loved. To Vin, that was like saying his mother hadn't mattered.

"Don't worry—I'll clean it up. Just call the agent so we can get it sold. Then you won't have to worry about it any longer."

His father spun around and stalked back to the house. Then he turned back to face his son. "Do you think I want to look at it that way?" he asked. "Did it ever occur to you that if it sold, I'd have to see someone running it, day in and day out?" He reached for the door.

Vin sighed. This was a no-win situation for his dad. "I know. But wouldn't you rather see someone care for it than… that?" he pressed.

His dad nodded. "Okay. I'll call the agent and see if she can come over tomorrow." He pulled the door closed with more force than necessary. It was the most fire Vin had seen from his dad yet.

Now that he'd gotten some rest, he had energy, so he grabbed his keys and wallet from inside and headed out to the hardware store. He might as well grab the things he was going to need and get started. And who knew? Maybe his father would even decide to help.

VIN STARTED by fixing the wonky shutter on the house so it hung straight, and did a few other things that needed attention. One of the stair treads needed fixing, and he got it tight once again. He also pulled out some of the weeds from the garden in front of the house and figured that at some point, he'd get some flowers and mulch to spruce it up. It was as if his dad didn't care about anything anymore. It bothered him to see his dad slowing down, and the house, shabby and neglected, seemed to mirror his state of mind. Vin's parents had always kept the house in immaculate shape and the yard full of color. The least he could do was try to bring it back to life.

"Looks nice," his dad said, offering the first real smile Vin had seen from him since he'd arrived. "It's getting on to dinner."

"Then let's go to the Springs." It would be good to get his father away from the house, and maybe they could talk… about something… anything. "I'll get cleaned up and then we can go." He put the tools back in the shed and closed the door, and after he'd washed his hands, he and his dad headed to the family-owned restaurant that he knew his dad really liked.

His father sat in the passenger seat, looking out the window, saying nothing until they had almost reached their destination. "Do you have plans? Things you want to do while you're here?"

"I thought we could spend some time together," Vin suggested. It had been over six years since he'd been home, and his last visit had been difficult, to say the least. His mother had been gone six months, and Vin had been concerned about his dad. He'd come home just in time to find out that his dad had closed the business and was putting it up for sale. The building and greenhouse had sat empty for that long.

"Not sure why you want to do that. I'm not exciting. There are no movie stars or famous people for you to hobnob with around here. It's not like LA. Nothing exciting ever happens here."

Little did his dad guess that there weren't that many stars or famous people in LA either. At least, not like Vin had expected when he'd hightailed it out town after having his heart shattered. Visions of becoming the florist to the stars just hadn't quite worked the way he'd thought. At one point he had thought he was on his way, but an economic downturn had ripped that out of his grasp. Even the gay scene that he had embraced so fully when he'd first arrived, trying to bury the pain under acres of sex and men, had lost its luster. In truth, what Vin wanted was closer to what his parents had had—someone to love him and a family of his own. But he was no longer sure he was going to find it in LA… or anywhere. Maybe his one chance had already passed him by.

"I don't meet many movie stars. I just design and arrange flowers for them. Though we did deliver flowers to Marilyn Monroe's grave a few weeks ago." He pulled in and found a parking space. "What I do out there is kind of exciting, though. People there always seem to want something new and different. That means that every day, I get to create and make something I've never tried before. I find that exciting." Not that he was knocking what his mom and dad had done. They'd built a business on simple arrangements, locally made gifts, and beautiful flowers that either of his parents would be happy to take to any occasion. If it hadn't met that standard, then they hadn't sold it. Things had been that simple. And that business had afforded them all a decent living.

"Do you own the shop now?" his dad asked. "Last time you were home, you said you thought the owner was going to sell."

"She's trying. But there's no way I can afford it. And from the looks of it, neither can anyone else. So while the place is still technically on the market, we're just going on as usual." It was a shame. His dream had always been to own his own place. He saved every month so he could get closer to that dream, but he just didn't have enough money put away.

"At least you're still working. That's always good." His father got out of the car, and Vin followed him into the restaurant, where the girl behind the counter greeted him by name and showed him to a table right away.

"That's Lesley. She's a sweetheart. Her family own this place—they bought it when the old owners retired last year—and she works here after school. The whole family does. Her brother works in the kitchen, and her father is the manager." His dad seemed happy as a steady stream of people passed by and greeted him. It seemed that his dad was still a social animal—just not when his son was around.

"How often do you come here?" Vin asked, deciding on the chicken pot pie.

"Two or three times a week, I guess. It's so much easier than trying to make a meal for just me. Your mother was the one who was good in the kitchen.

The food here tastes much better than anything I could make," he said with a slight grimace.

Once they'd both made their selections, the server took their orders, then lingered a few moments to talk with his dad.

"Hey, Vin. I didn't know you were back in town."

Vin's heart gave a little shudder. He knew that voice. Turning, he looked up at Casey Lombard, whose smile was the same one Vin remembered from when they were sixteen and got in trouble for… well, just about anything they thought they could get away with.

"I got in today. I worked ahead at the shop so I could take some time off to visit Dad." Vin hadn't seen Casey since the funeral. "How are Alicia and little Brianna?" His dad had told him about Casey's daughter, but Vin had never met her.

"Alicia returned to the Costa Rica to be with her family a few years ago," Casey said softly.

Vin didn't know what to say to that. Sure, he was sorry, for Casey's sake, that things hadn't worked out, but he couldn't help being glad that the woman was gone. There'd just been something about her that he didn't trust.

"Things between the two of us had been… bad. Our marriage had pretty much been a mistake right from the beginning, I guess… with the exception of Brianna." He scratched his head. "It was ugly. In fact, the ugliness really started shortly after you left for LA." He seemed miserable. "Alicia is now fighting for custody of Brianna. She wants to take her to Costa Rica to live with her family and is trying to drag me into dealing with the courts down there. Thankfully, the authorities here have denied all her petitions to have Brianna sent down there. Bri is an American citizen, and the courts here believe, as I do, that if Brianna left the country, Alicia's family would never allow her to return."

"So you have her?" He could definitely see Casey as a parent. He'd always been the one to watch out for him and the other kids on the playground.

"Yes. But I'm getting tired of fighting. I have told Alicia she's welcome to come here and see Bri. Hell, I even agreed to pay for the plane ticket. But she's refused, which hasn't helped her case." There was a slight sparkle in Casey's eyes. "I want my daughter to have a relationship with her mother, but not at the expense of her—and my—happiness. Brianna goes to school here, she has friends and family here. There's no way in hell that I'm going to uproot—" He cut himself off. "Sorry. I tend to go on about this."

"Daddy!" Speaking of cuteness. Brianna hurried over to his side from the nearby table. "The waitress brought the food and it's getting cold." She took Casey's hand. "You need to eat."

"I'm staying at Dad's," Vin said. He fished in his wallet, pulled out one of his business cards, and handed it to Casey. "It has my cell number on it. Maybe we can get together while I'm in town."

"Sure." Casey took the card, looked at it for a moment, then let Brianna pull him away.

Vin watched them go, a lump in his throat. Casey had been his very first crush in high school, and damned if he hadn't fallen hard. Then, for Vin, during their college years their friendship had grown even deeper, into something resembling love.

Vin mentally shook himself. While it was natural that he'd react this way to seeing Casey again, he'd be smart to push those painful memories away. What they'd had was over long ago.

They'd been just a couple of stupid kids who couldn't be open and honest with each other. Casey hadn't been willing to acknowledge their relationship, and Vin hadn't been willing to hide. When Casey had started seeing Alicia, it had hurt Vin—badly. But he was still willing to wait, hoping that Casey would realize what they had and come back to him. Only it hadn't worked out that way.

The day after Vin's mother died, Casey had admitted to him that Alicia was pregnant. It had just been too much. Just thinking about trying to live without his mom—and suddenly Casey too—had been more than he could take. He had to leave town as quickly as he could.

Vin had a distant cousin who lived in LA, and he'd decided that the West Coast was as good a place as any to start a new life. He'd had a whole new future ahead of him. And while he'd done some good work in LA, nothing seemed to matter as much as this man from his past who moved toward the table right in front of him, looking more amazing than Vin remembered. Casey had only grown more handsome with time. "See you later."

Brianna led Casey back to their table as their own food arrived. "Do you see Casey much?" Vin couldn't help glancing at where Casey sat.

His dad shook his head. "Every now and then. But I'm an old fart, and he's young and just building a life, like you. It isn't like we travel in the same circles." His dad started eating right away.

"Have you seen the doctor lately?"

His father set down his fork. "Why would you ask that? Of course I have, and I'm healthy as a horse. Are you trying to figure out how soon I'm going to kick the bucket or something?" His overreaction told Vin a lot.

"I was trying to make conversation, since you're so determined not to say much." He took a few bites of his dinner. No one out in California made proper pot pie, and this was so good. "But since you mention it, why are you being defensive?" He leaned a little closer. "What are you hiding?"

"It's nothing," he groused.

"If it's nothing, then tell me about it." Vin was determined to get him to open up.

"The doctor has me on pills for my blood sugar. He says that I need to lose twenty or thirty pounds. I've been this weight for years. Still, he says that maybe I won't need the pills if I diet. Says I need to take a walk every day too."

"I bet he didn't tell you to eat hamburgers and chips two or three times a week," Vin pressed. "Dad, you need to take better care of yourself. We've already lost Mom." He left the rest of that thought unsaid. The truth was that his father was the only family Vin had left.

"Where am I supposed to walk?"

"There's the rail trail that runs behind the middle school. It starts at the end of the block. It's shaded and really pretty as it winds by the spring run." It made sense to him. Vin had taken up going to the gym a few days a week some time ago. He realized he needed some regular exercise, and going to the beach on a regular basis wasn't practical for him.

"I'll think about it." His father's grumpiness was back full force, and he leaned over the table to eat his food, signaling that he was tired of this topic. Not that Vin had any intention of letting it drop permanently.

"Are there any women you're interested in?" Vin loved the expression of shock on this father's face.

"Now you're just being a pain in the ass. Knock it off."

Vin shrugged. "Then say something that I don't have to try to drag out of you."

His father sighed. "Fine. Sometimes I visit with Louise Brouges. She lost her husband three years ago. I'm sure you remember her." Vin definitely did. Louise made the best chocolate chip cookies on the planet and baklava to die for. Maybe she'd bring some over while he was in town. "We go out for lunch every once in a while. Her kids are in Philadelphia now, and sometimes she gets lonely. We both do. She's an old friend and I'm not rotting away just sitting in this house. Now, is that enough of a heart-to-heart for you to leave me the hell alone for twenty minutes so I can eat and not get indigestion?"

"Okay. You know I was just trying to get under your skin." Yeah, he was probably being a bad son, but his father could be so closemouthed about things.

"You're a little shit, you know that?"

"Yup. I come by it naturally. Mom always said I got it from you." He grinned to himself and went back to his dinner.

"Are you going to pester me the entire time you're here? If you are, just go back to California and leave me alone." He finished his burger and drank his coffee.

"Of course. Why do you think I came home? It's been two years, and I haven't had anyone to pester, bug, cajole, nag, or push in that entire time. I think I'm going through withdrawal, and you're the cure." He smiled, and finally his dad broke a grin. "That's better. Your face didn't crack. Not even a little bit."

"Okay. Let's get this out in the open. Why did you come back, if it isn't to drive me around the bend? And don't tell me it's so you and I can reconnect or get to know each other as adults. That's a bunch of California New-Age horseshit if I ever heard it. I changed your diapers and taught you how to walk and how to ride a bike. You're my son, and I'm the one who took his life into his own hands and let you get behind the wheel of a car after your mother swore she'd never do that again as long as she lived." He took a sip of his coffee. "I went to every concert and soccer game. The whole gay thing threw me for a loop, but I accepted you for who you are and didn't act like other parents."

He set down his mug and glanced over to where Casey sat. Vin knew what his father hadn't needed to say. Casey's folks would never have accepted him the way Vin's parents had. "You're my son, and I already know you pretty well, especially when you're acting like a hemorrhoid on the ass of life." There was the father he knew. He thought that maybe the man he remembered had disappeared, that losing his mother had changed him forever.

Vin grinned and sat back, relieved to find that the father who had taken a six-hour road trip with him and some friends, entertaining them the entire time, was still in there somewhere. Maybe there was hope that his father was finally moving on after losing Mom. Maybe it was time for both of them.

"Mom used to say that about you," Vin said with a smile.

"And when she died, she left her pain-in-the-buttness to you in her will."

Vin chuckled and grinned. "I knew you were in there somewhere." He finished his pot pie and drank the last of his soda. The server brought them refills.

"Are you really going to clean up the florist shop?" His father's smile dimmed.

Vin shrugged. "Why not? If you want to sell it, then it needs to be in good repair. The way it is, there's no way any potential buyer would even consider it."

"No. I guess not," he whispered.

"You really don't want to sell it, do you?" Vin asked.

His dad shook his head. "But I'm not going to get what I want. What I want is to have your mother back so she and I can work in the shop again. She'd sit at her table and make flower arrangements that took your breath away. I'd stand at the register and greet the customers or stock the shelves with her looking over my shoulder, telling me where everything went." He let out a deep sigh. "We did that for forty years, and I want it back." He sipped his coffee. "But she's gone, and that can't possibly happen. So yeah, clean it up and let's make it look good again. Maybe then someone will buy it and fill the place with life. Your mother would have wanted that." He motioned, and the server came over. He spoke to her softly, handed her some money, and then stood up. "Let's go."

Vin finished his soda in a few gulps and followed his father out of the restaurant. This time the drive was quiet, but Vin understood why and let his father be alone with his thoughts. He parked in front of the house and got out of the car. His father went right inside. Vin wandered around the side of the house into the shadow of one of the large trees on the property. The sun had already set, and full darkness would be on them soon enough. Still, his body was on West Coast time, so it seemed early to him.

He wandered around back and stopped behind the house, looking at the greenhouse on the other side of the road just behind the house. Suddenly he saw a light flicker inside the building. Vin opened the back door and went into the house. He pulled the curtains just before his dad turned on the lights. "Turn them off."

"Why?"

"Dad, please. Just come here." He waited for the room to go dark and then parted the curtains. "Someone is in the greenhouse." He watched, seeing nothing for a minute, but then the lights danced low over the floor and the old display tables that lined the sides.

"I'll call the police," his dad said as Vin let the curtains fall back into place and went through the house locking all the doors.

CHAPTER 2

CASEY RECOGNIZED that address right away. He'd stopped to drop Brianna at his mother's place for the night, after they had story time at Hummingbird Books. Dex, the owner, had given in to popular demand and read one of the Officer Buckle stories, with his husband, Les, playing the title character in one of his old uniforms. Les had been a colleague and a friend before he'd been injured and had to leave the force. It was good to see him and have a few minutes to catch up before Les's young fans demanded his attention.

Casey had already changed and was on his way into work when the call came through. He responded that he would take it. They were understaffed that evening, so the dispatcher was grateful that he wouldn't have to find someone on short notice. Less than five minutes after the call, Casey approached the house. He parked out front and knocked on the door.

"Yes?" Vin answered. He'd know that voice anywhere.

"Police," he said quietly, and the door opened. Vin stared at him. Casey's throat went dry just seeing Vin again, and he swallowed hard so he could speak.

"Case…. When did you become a cop?" Vin pushed the door open farther and let him in.

At times Casey was just as surprised as Vin seemed to be about his choice of career. Casey had had other dreams when he and Vin were kids. At one point Casey had wanted to be a doctor. God, he remembered how he and Vin used to talk about everything in the tent they'd pitched out in his backyard. He and Vin had hatched their plan to toilet paper the principal's brand-new car in middle school there, and they'd planned the most epic bike ride in history… until Vin's mother had caught wind of their plans to ride to New York City to see the ball drop on New Year's Eve when they were thirteen. Looking back, Vin had always been the one with big ideas, and Casey had been the one to figure out how to make them happen. Too bad he hadn't figured out how not to get caught. He and Vin had shared their dreams, their hopes for the future—including the fact that Casey hadn't wanted to become a policeman like his father and grandpa. He'd wanted to do something else. But just like so many other things in his life, Casey had given up what he'd wanted in favor of what was expected of him.

His father was a cop, his grandpa was a cop, and he was expected to become one too. And as usual, rather than fight them, he had just gone along.

Casey cleared his throat. "How about one question at a time. What's going on?" There wasn't time for a personal history. He was here on a call, and as much as he wanted to sit down and catch up with Vin, he had a job to do.

"The flower shop and greenhouse have been shut up since Mom died. But when Dad and I got home, I looked out the back door and saw lights flashing in the greenhouse, as if someone was in there with flashlights." Vin rocked slightly from foot to foot, obviously worried, while Mack sat in his chair watching reruns of *The Nanny*. It was an interesting dichotomy.

"He's been peeking out those curtains for the last fifteen minutes," Mack added. "That's why the lights are off now.

"But they were there. Dad saw them too." He took a deep breath and shook his head. "I don't get it. I checked out the store earlier today, and it was closed up tight. It didn't look as if anyone had been in there. But I never thought to check around the back of the greenhouse. Maybe someone broke one of the panes of glass and got in that way." Vin peered out the window once again. "There are no lights now. It's as if I imagined them…."

"You didn't," Mack said. "I saw them too. But it's probably just kids getting into trouble the way you two used to do. In the morning we can go investigate."

Casey wasn't so sure. This situation was beginning to have a familiar feel. Lights after dark in an out-of-the-way location that wasn't being used. He'd seen this before, and it was becoming a bigger problem with each passing week. "Is there power in the building?"

Mack sighed. "It's been turned off here at the house. If you want to play Columbo, you'll have to go out to the store and turn the power on. The main breaker was shut off once we closed the business down. I locked the box, so you'll need the key." He got up slowly, then walked into the kitchen, opened a drawer, and pulled out a key. He handed it to Casey.

"Thanks," Casey said. "I'm going to call for another unit, and we'll go in and check it out. You two stay here and keep the doors locked. This shouldn't take very long."

"The breaker box is in the office area behind the counter. Just unlock it and flip the main switch. You should be able to turn on the store and greenhouse lights, if the bulbs still work."

Casey tilted his head to the side and answered a radio call. "Okay. I'll be back," he said, leaving the house.

He'd only been outside a few minutes when Red and Carter pulled up in their police cruiser.

Red was a huge man who'd been in an accident as a kid. He was a great guy, but his facial scars made him seem intimidating. Carter, on the other hand, was the department's resident computer expert. Together, the two officers made a formidable team. Casey knew them the way he knew all the cops at the station, but not as well as he probably should have. He had felt like an outsider for much of his life, and that feeling had carried over into his work. It wasn't them—it was him. Unfortunately, he didn't have a clue what to do about it.

After discussing the situation, the three of them drove to the closed florist business and shone their flashlights around the area before peering inside the building. Casey's beam of light pierced the darkness, but only dust floated through it. When he didn't see anything, he used the key to unlock the door.

"I'll cover you," Red said as Casey entered the shop. It was totally quiet. He moved carefully around the place, past the old counter, and walked toward the back room, shining his light everywhere, including on the electric box. He unlocked it and flipped on the power. Nothing happened. Casey checked the breakers, ensuring they were all on.

Light blazed on behind him. "Helps if you turn on the switch," Red said, half teasing.

Casey closed the electrical box as more lights flipped on, illuminating the work area and the greenhouse behind it. Carter and Red checked out the shop. Then they all moved into the greenhouse.

"This is supposed to be empty?" Red asked, pointing to a forest of green clustered in the center of the greenhouse, sheltered by the racks on either side.

"Yes," Casey said. "I was just speaking to the owners. Mack closed everything up after his wife died." He drew closer and sniffed, recognizing the scent.

"Well, this is quite interesting," Carter said softly. "It seems our widowed retiree is supplementing his income." He made a radio call to explain their findings.

"I doubt Mack would be growing marijuana and then report seeing lights so we could investigate and find his plants. Think about it. It's more likely that someone has been using the deserted greenhouse as a place to keep some illicit crops, just like we've seen in other small locations over the last three months. Only these plants aren't as well cared for."

Catching these people was like trying to harness the tide. Every time the police found a location and thought they were close, the perps seemed to melt away. "We need to call the chief, let him know what we found, and ask how he wants to proceed," Casey said. Red nodded, and Carter just grimaced, as if embarrassed that he'd jumped to such an obviously wrong conclusion.

As Casey pulled out his phone, Carter made his way down the side of the twenty-five or so struggling plants at the far end of the greenhouse. "Wait," he called out.

"What did you find?" Red shouted. Casey stopped dialing.

"You guys gotta see this," Carter yelled.

Casey made his way down the aisle with Red, careful not to touch anything. Carter pointed to a series of small plastic containers on the floor, about forty of them, each one labeled and numbered. Once they'd all pulled on gloves, he opened the lid of one of them. It held a few boxes. Carter carefully picked one up, opened it, and pulled out a bottle of OxyContin. Another box in the same tub contained Percocet. "Prescription-type opiates." They'd been seeing a lot of these in town lately, along with the usual illicit substances. The opioid drug crisis had created a lot of potential customers.

"Look how they're numbered."

"It looks like a warehousing system of some sort," Red said. "Or an order system." He opened the other boxes, which were also numbered but empty. "I'd guess that these orders have already been picked up. This one must be awaiting delivery."

Carter nodded and placed the lid back on the container. Then they all made their way back to the florist shop area, leaving the rest of the boxes where they were.

Casey took a minute to phone the chief, explaining what they'd found and asking what he wanted them to do going forward.

"How much is there?" the chief asked.

"Maybe a couple dozen plants. They aren't mature yet—only about two feet in height or so—but they're not doing well. I think whoever is behind this has shifted their focus. They've turned this location into some sort of distribution point. Not all the containers are full."

"Then leave them and have Red and Carter plant motion sensor cameras inside. Let's use the place as bait. If we're lucky, we'll catch ourselves a dealer or two. Do you think the owners are involved?"

"Considering they called us…." Casey let him draw his own conclusion.

"Right. Then get their permission and tell them to stay away from the place for a few days. I want to get these guys." Chief Robertson was getting pissed, and Casey wished he'd let one of the other guys make this call. He was well aware that whenever they made inroads into this ring of people who were growing pot around town, they evaporated and disappeared like fog. Up until recently, it hadn't been a top priority. But the chief was getting pressured to find the perps, and as of this moment, the crime had just escalated from being a nuisance to something much bigger. "Let's set a little trap and see if we don't catch someone."

"All right. We'll get it set up," Casey said, though it was likely pointless. Chances were that the dealers were already aware that their location had been discovered. They'd abandon it like they had all the others and shift operations to other locations. That was the hardest part about trying to catch these guys. Instead of a commanding a large operation somewhere in the country, they set up a number of small locations that usually escaped notice. When one was found, they moved on with minimal loss. The multitude of other locations likely more than covered for the ones that were abandoned. And Casey figured the perps would do the same thing here. Though maybe that wouldn't be the case this time. There was a hell of a lot more money involved in illicit drugs than there was in a few pot plants.

"Do that." And with that, the chief ended the call.

Casey relayed the message, and after securing permission from Mack, they all got started. Casey and Red pulled out the equipment, and Carter got to work setting up the camera. He placed it high off the ground so it couldn't be easily reached. Then they turned out the lights, locked up, and left things pretty much the way they'd found them. When they got back to the car, Red and Carter got another call, and Casey returned to the house.

"You found *what* in my greenhouse?" Mack asked, his eyes wide in shock. Vin, on the other hand, was nearly laughing. Casey hadn't told them about the hard drugs yet. He wanted to gauge their reactions first.

"I live in California. A small number of plants in a closed-up greenhouse would barely register on anyone's radar. They're more concerned about growers clearing acres of protected forest. Besides, it's pretty much legal there unless it's on federal land, so this sort of thing isn't all that big a deal."

"It's not legal here, though. And so we find these little growing operations in the area every so often. But this is worse than that. It seems someone is using your greenhouse as a distribution center for harder drugs." He paused, seeing the color drain from their faces as shock set in. *That* was the reaction he'd been hoping for. "We'd like you both to just stay away from the shop and greenhouse for a while. We're hoping we'll be able to catch someone who'll help us get to the bottom of this." Casey sighed. "I'd really appreciate your cooperation. I have a feeling this is just the break we've been looking for."

Slippery bastards. Casey really wanted to nail these guys. He'd seen how opiate addiction could decimate a small town. And if he solved this…? Well, maybe he'd feel like a real cop for a change. If he busted these drug dealers, he'd finally fit in with the other guys. At least he hoped he would.

"I get it, and I'm sorry," Vin told him genuinely. "How did they get in?"

"Looks like they jimmied the greenhouse door. We left it the way it was. Hopefully they won't realize they've been discovered or damage something else trying to get inside. We'll give it a few days and see what happens."

"So you want us to just stay away from the shop and greenhouse for a couple of days. That's all?" Vin asked, his shoulders slumping. "You know Dad is trying to sell the place. I'd planned to fix both places up so they would show better to potential buyers. This is going to change things." Vin narrowed his gaze. "You said just a few days, right?"

"Yes. They may already know they've been made and abandon their operation or make a play to get their stock out. If they don't, then we'll remove everything in a few days. Hopefully they don't know and we'll bust them. Either way, the plants will be removed." He smiled. "There's a lot of work to be done in there. The place is a mess. It wasn't like the dealers were particularly careful. They moved things around, and there's potting soil and dirt on every flat surface."

"Great," Vin said softly.

"If you want some help, I'm available. I'm off Wednesday and Thursday, and we should know the state of things by then." Casey wrote his cell number on the back of one of his cards and handed it to Vin.

"Give me a call." He smiled and his heart skipped a beat when Vin met his gaze for a few seconds. Vin had these great eyes when his smile was warm and full. Casey loved that.

He was finally starting to put his life in order and get himself on a track that felt right. For too many years, Casey had tried to conform to his family's expectations. He hadn't gone against their wishes, and he regretted that now. Casey had married and given his parents a granddaughter. It should have been perfect. But none of it had felt real, not back then. He'd felt like he was just acting a role in a play. It had taken Casey a long time to realize that he had become a spectator in his own life. When Alicia left, he'd taken a long, hard look at his life, and he hadn't liked what he'd seen. He'd thought he'd been a good husband to Alicia, a good father to Brianna. But considering the way Alicia left, maybe not.

"Casey?" Vin prompted.

Casey startled, realizing his mind had taken a huge flight of fancy while he was still standing with Vin. "Sorry." He pulled his thoughts to where they needed to be, on the present instead of on his rather pathetic past. "Like I said, call if you need some help. And I'll be in touch about what's going on with the crops in the greenhouse. Just give it a few days."

Vin shrugged. "I guess I don't have much choice. But thanks for everything. We'll stay away, but if we see anything, I'll be sure to let you know. As for the help, don't be surprised if I take you up on it. I think that place is going to need more work than one person can manage."

Casey nodded, then headed out the door. Once outside, he radioed in to let the dispatcher know he was free, then got back in his car and took a deep breath. After all these years, being around Vin could still make his head spin.

OVER THE next few days, Casey and Carter checked the cameras but found nothing. No one came back, and they could make out just enough of the plants in the distance to see them wilt and then slump in the heat without any water. It was clear that whoever was using the greenhouse had abandoned the location. "Chief, I'm going to clear out the cache of drugs and pot from the greenhouse and bring it in as evidence."

"I'll call the DEA to alert them to the situation." The chief was obviously disappointed but not surprised. They had suspected this would happen. Still, some days it seemed they couldn't catch a break.

"Thanks. I'm going to head over now. I should be finished before I leave for the day." He left the office and checked out one of the SUVs. Then he drove through town and out to the south side and pulled up in front of the old florist shop. The place did indeed seem forlorn. It was a shame. Casey remembered it as a place that was always vibrant, decorated with the seasons, and filled with flowers. His mother used to get all of her plants there each spring. And it had been in the shop that Casey had first met Vin all those years ago. They had become best friends and had had each other's back all through school. Until….

"Thought you might need these," Vin said as he came up behind Casey and handed him the set of keys. "You left them on the table the last time you were here. I kept them handy in case you needed them again." He sighed gently. "Sometimes things change so much, we barely recognize them." He turned to Casey, and Casey wondered if Vin was talking about the shop… or him.

"I know," Casey said softly. "I can still see your mother standing behind that work table of hers, offering a smile to everyone who came through the door." Now the front of the building was streaked with dirt and the windows filthy, with spiders taking up residence under the porch.

"Me too. I miss her a lot." Vin sighed. "Can I ask what happened between you and your wife?"

Casey had come a long way in the past few years, but this part was still the hardest. "I tried to make a go of it. I really did. But in the end, I think she figured out that she wasn't what I needed. No woman would be what I needed." There, he'd said it.

Vin shifted his attention to him, his mouth hanging open slightly. "You're attracted to men?"

The way Vin said it told Casey that he understood. Casey had struggled for years trying to find a place where he fit. He didn't identify as gay, but he liked men. Maybe he was bisexual, or maybe he was just different. For him, it wasn't that simple. He nodded slowly and thoughtfully. He really hadn't expected to have this conversation—not standing out in front of the old flower shop.

Especially when he should be working. "Let's see what we have inside."

Casey unlocked the door and went inside first. He checked over the shop before letting Vin follow him.

"This looks the same as I remember. It's just a lot dirtier." Vin ran his hand over the old work table that his mother had used for all those years. "I'll stay in here while you take care of what you need to," he told Casey.

"Thanks." Casey continued on into the greenhouse, where the wilted plants now sat dying on the floor and the bins sat where they'd left them. He pulled on gloves and checked them over more carefully, then lifted the plastic trays and began carrying them out. He placed them in the back of the SUV. He hoped that he might be able to get some information from the containers or the equipment he found. Once he had everything, Casey got large plastic bags, shoved the remaining plants inside, and stacked the pots and trays. Then he logged each container, noting all the numbers and contents before sliding them into the back of his vehicle.

"Is that all?" Vin asked.

"Yeah. I bagged up the plants and have everything else locked in the back of police vehicle. I want to make one more pass, and then the place is yours once more." Casey was glad this was over and that Vin was going to do something with the building. "I can almost feel your mom here."

Vin chuckled. "Yeah. She loved this space and the way she had things set up in it. It was perfect for all the arrangements she put together for weddings, funerals, and everything else in between. It's where she taught me all she knew and encouraged me to experiment with my own style." He slapped his hands to get the dust off. "She was the one who encouraged me to take floral design classes."

"Do you think she wanted you to take over for her?" Casey asked. It seemed like a natural fit, at least to him.

"I know that was what Dad had hoped for." Vin hesitated. "But when she passed, things here changed for me. I needed to find my own way." The lingering hurt in Vin's eyes told Casey that a lot of that change had been instigated by him. And he really couldn't blame Vin for leaving. Casey had made decisions back then that had cost him dearly.

"I had family living in LA," Vin continued. "It seemed like a good place to try to make a fresh start." He seemed far away.

"It sounds to me like maybe you're second-guessing that," Casey said.

"Maybe a little. But I couldn't just take over for my mother. If I had tried, everyone would have expected me to do things the way she did and to make the same kind of arrangements. That wasn't what I wanted. I guess I needed a chance to prove myself, to find my own style. I needed to know who I was and what I could do. You know?"

Casey understood that feeling. He was just starting to let the real Casey out to play. And the freedom it offered was intoxicating.

Casey checked the greenhouse area and then told Vin that the coast was clear. He could start the cleanup. Casey had what he needed.

"I'll be working out here tomorrow," Vin said. "Were you serious about helping?"

Casey smiled. "I'll be here." He couldn't help the burst of excitement he felt at seeing Vin again. They had been friends for years, and Vin would be going back to Los Angeles in about a week, so that flutter in his belly couldn't be anything more than basic animalistic attraction. It had been too long to be anything else.

Besides, although he'd accepted the fact that he was attracted to men, it wasn't something he was prepared to act on. Casey told himself he wasn't in the closet. He just hadn't been comfortable acting on his feelings, so he never had. There'd been no reason to. He hadn't found anybody he wanted to be with, and he knew his family would have a hard time accepting it… if they ever did. He had been married to Alicia for seven years, and they had had Brianna. Starting to come to grips with who he was had been the first step. Now he had to figure out how to explain things to his daughter.

"I appreciate the help and the company," Vin told him and extended his hand. "Thanks. And I'm sorry about all of this. I suppose if Dad had kept a closer eye on things, this might not have happened."

"I'm glad to help. On my off hours, it's usually just Brianna and me." He often felt like he didn't belong. Maybe it was because he was a single dad with responsibilities, or just because he wasn't as driven, but he sometimes felt like he didn't quite belong anywhere. The only time he had felt like he'd been in the right place at the right time was when he'd been with Vin. He'd been a part of a true friendship, but he'd managed to mess that up years ago. But seeing Vin again brought him right back to those times. And he wasn't a kid any longer. Casey had come a long way in coming to terms with himself and what he really wanted.

Vin chuckled. "And since you'll be off duty, I think I can arrange for all the beer and pizza you could possibly want."

Casey groaned at Vin's wicked smile. "You remember that?"

"Yeah. We were both troublemakers—really stupid ones. But yeah. I figured now that we're legal, we can have what we want… and we'll know when to quit." He laughed. "I'll see you tomorrow. And thanks. You really don't have to do this."

"What are friends for?" He handed Vin back the keys and headed out to his car. His spirit was lighter than it had been in a long time. Maybe spending time with his old friend would be good for him. Vin made some of the questions and worries he was dealing with a little easier to face. He was someone Casey could be himself around. They had known each other since they were kids, and there was no pressure to fall into bed… or anything else. That Vin made Casey's belly flutter and his temperature rise? Those were just physical reactions that he could easily push aside. After all, he'd been doing that sort of thing for a long time.

Casey started the car and pushed his unwanted thoughts from his mind.

Once he'd sort of figured out what was going on with himself, Casey had made some decisions. He had been faithful to Alicia, and he did the best he could in his marriage because he had made a promise, and he kept his promises. Alicia had been the one to leave. And now Casey had Brianna, and he would do whatever was best for her. That meant that he needed to be careful about who he let into his life. Vin was great, but he wasn't staying.

Which pretty well told Casey what he needed to do. And he hated it.

"DADDY!" BRIANNA said the following morning, sitting at Casey's mother's kitchen table. "Grandma made blueberry pancakes." She grinned as she ate. They were her favorite food in the whole world.

"That's great, honey." He kissed the top of her head, and his mother handed him a big mug of coffee and a plate of what she knew was also his favorite breakfast.

"What time did you get done with your shift?" she asked. "It must have been late."

Casey nodded. "Midnight. Then I went right home and got some sleep. I just need a few minutes to wake up. Once this munchkin and I finish the best breakfast ever, she and I can be on our way. I know you have plans today." His mom had a garden-tending session in one of the parks with her garden club, and Casey had long ago learned not to interfere with those ladies. They were sweet but ferocious.

"Sit," she commanded. Then her expression softened. "Eat. There's time." His mother had changed very little over the years. Her hair was gray, but she still had the same sharp eyes and ready smile, with a touch of recrimination for anything that didn't mesh with her worldview just below the surface. Casey didn't argue and sat down with his daughter. His mother definitely wasn't the kind to shower her family with hugs and kisses, but with food? That was another matter. It had taken him years to figure that out.

"What are we doing today, Daddy? Can we go to the park? I want to see the ducks and geese." She swallowed her last bite, then took her plate and glass to the sink the way she'd been taught. Brianna was a rule follower, which was a relief sometimes. But she could be a rule enforcer with everyone else.

"Yes, we can." He paused. "But when we're done here, we're going to go home. I need you to put on some old clothes. Today we're going to help an old friend of mine. He needs some cleaning done, and we're going to help. He even says there will be all the pizza we can eat for lunch." That got a smile out of the child.

His mother put her hands on her hips. "I can't believe you're going to have your daughter working that way." The look she gave him intimated that he was the worst parent on earth.

"Brianna is learning about money. It's important that she knows where it comes from and how to earn it." Not that he expected Vin to pay either of them, but he'd see to it that Brianna was rewarded for help-ing. "You remember Vin? His parents had the flower shop off Ridge Street. The place is a mess, and he wants to get it ready to sell. So I volunteered to help. If Brianna comes along, she can help too… and earn some money at the same time."

"I'll help." Lately Brianna had her eye on a game for her Switch. This would be a way for her to earn some money to put toward it, and help some-one else at the same time. "I'll get my cleaning stuff from home." She was already excited. Casey's heart warmed. She was a great kid. His daughter was learning the value of work and money, and that was important to him. But she also had a soft heart, and that was even more important.

"Really," his mother humphed. "Brianna can come with me and help. We'll be there for about an hour. She doesn't need to be doing hard labor."

Brianna turned to him. "But I want pizza. And I'm big enough to help. Really, I am." She pooched out her lower lip before standing straight and tall. "If I save my money, maybe I can get a puppy. Right, Daddy?"

He shook his head. "What did we say about that, Brianna? You're too young to look after a puppy right now." He finished his breakfast and decided to ignore his mother's statement about his daughter. Sometimes his mom worried that Brianna was growing up too fast. But Brianna was *his* daughter. "Get your things and we'll head home to change clothes."

Casey took his plate to the sink and kissed his mom's cheek. "Thank you for taking her last night."

By the time he got to the door, Brianna was already there with her overnight bag. As they walked out to the car, Brianna yelled over her shoulder, "Thank you, Grandma," then jumped into her booster seat. He drove them home to get ready for their day.

"Is THAT it?" Brianna asked when they pulled up in front of the florist shop.

"Yup." He opened the door when Vin came over. Then he popped the trunk and unlocked the doors so Brianna could get out. "This is Vin. He and I have been friends since we were boys, just a little older than you."

"Hi," Vin said with a smile. Brianna said hello as well and held out her hand for Vin to shake it. Sometimes she was such a grown-up little lady, and that scared him. She was changing so fast. Soon enough she wouldn't need him anymore. "Are you here to help too?"

Brianna nodded. "Daddy said there would be pizza."

Vin grinned. "There will be so much that you'll have to be careful that your belly doesn't burst." He straightened up and met Casey's gaze with a smile. The air around them suddenly grew warmer.

"I've got cleaning stuff in the trunk," Brianna piped up.

Vin held out his hand to her. "Then let's go get it. I have the perfect job for you."

Brianna took it, and just like that, she and Vin were off. They got her stuff, and Casey followed them inside.

"How about you clean off this table for me? My mama used to work there all the time."

"My mama is in Costa Rica." The tone she used was the same one she might use to tell him she'd brushed her teeth that night. Reporting a fact, nothing more. That made Casey sad, because Brianna needed to know her mother. She asked about her sometimes, but the longer Alicia was gone, the less connection Brianna had with her.

"You know, this place is pretty dirty," Vin said to the girl. "You might need to use something stronger than what you brought. But we should start with soap and water and see how that works." When she nodded, not put off at all, Vin explained what he wanted Brianna to do, and she got right to it. Then Vin turned to Casey. "I thought we would work in here first, then tackle the greenhouse later."

"Sounds good." Casey got a broom and began lightly sweeping the ceiling. Dust and cobwebs rained down on them. Brianna squealed and brushed her hair.

"Daddy…." Then she let out a long-suffering sigh.

"We're going to get dirty, honey. It's okay," Casey told her, then continued brushing the ceiling. Vin set to work on the windows and doors, and when he was finished with the ceilings, Casey began wiping down the old displays.

"Did your daddy ever tell you about the time he and I came home covered in mud?" Vin asked

Brianna. When she shook her head, he continued. "See, we went down to the creek over by the baseball field, looking for frogs."

"Grandma hates frogs," Brianna chirped. She was perched on the stool that had probably belonged to Vin's mother, and was carefully but thoroughly wiping down the surface of the worktable.

"That's why we were looking for them. We were going to put one in your grandma's pond. We wanted to scare her," Casey said.

"Why?" Brianna asked. "That seems mean."

Casey shrugged. "We were boys, and you know your grandma can be a little…."

"Grumpy," Vin supplied, and Brianna put her hand over her mouth as she giggled and nodded. "So we were looking for these frogs, and your daddy stepped in a mud hole—a really deep one. I tried to stop him from slipping, but he grabbed me and we both fell in." Vin's gaze shifted from Brianna to Casey. That smile—the mischievous one he'd seen so many times on his friend over the years—made his throat catch. "Your daddy and I were covered in stinky black mud. We managed to get out and up on the bank… and then we saw it." His voice had a deep, mysterious timbre to it, as if he was telling a ghost story. "The biggest frog we ever saw was sitting right there, looking at us. You know what he did?" Vin asked.

Brianna shook her head, and Casey found himself on edge, waiting too. "What?"

"He turned and hopped off." Vin jumped, Brianna squealed, and Casey grinned as his old friend and would be pretty with pink and purple." She seemed to know what she liked. "Why is there a refrigerator like that?"

"To keep the flowers fresh." The one thing he hadn't touched was the cooler. It hadn't been run in years, and he wasn't sure it would work. "I need to wash the glass, and then we can see if it will cool." He hoped so. Repairs would cost quite a bit, and while he was expecting to put some elbow grease into this, he hoped he wouldn't have to drop a bunch of cash too. Still, if everything worked, then it could be advertised that way. "Do you want to spray?" He handed her the window cleaner and let her go to town with it before he wiped down the doors.

"The outside looks good, and the windows are clean," Casey said. "I was going to continue on to the greenhouse and hose it down."

"Let's finish this and see if the refrigerator works," Vin said.

"I can do that," Casey said as Vin finished the outside of the doors.

"Great." Brianna sprayed the inside while Vin went in the back room to figure out which switch ran the cooler. He found it, and when he turned it on, the compressor hummed to life. He let out a deep breath of relief. Thank God! When he came back out front, Casey was closing the door.

"The air is cold," Brianna said holding her hand up. "That's good, right?"

"It's really good." It meant that the equipment was all in working order. Now all he needed was for the agent to sell the place.

Vin pulled out his phone and placed an order for pizza, soda, breadsticks, and even cookies for dessert, which earned him smiles from both Casey and Brianna.

"How about we close these doors to keep the cold in? Then we should wash up so we'll be ready to dig in when the food gets here." Casey carried a giggling Brianna outside, and Vin followed them with his gaze. Damn, Casey was gorgeous—his eyes sparkling, lips curled upward, laughing with his daughter. As Vin watched, an old longing bubbled to life. After all this time, Vin had never thought he would run into Casey again. And then to find out that he was gay—or at least that he had feelings for men…. Vin didn't quite know what to think.

He wondered if Casey had felt something for him when they were younger. Maybe that was the reason their friendship had faded and changed.

Vin watched his two helpers play together through the door, then called his dad. "Pizza is on the way. They're going to deliver it to the shop."

"Okay." His dad sounded a little down.

"Come on back and join us. That way you'll be able to take a look at what we've done." Once his father agreed, though halfheartedly, Vin ended the call just as another one came in. Vin confirmed where he wanted the delivery and stepped outside. He waved as the driver pulled up.

The man got out of his car and went to the back to pull out Vin's order. He looked at the shop, his eyes assessing the work they'd done. "This is cool.

"There's no rule book for parenting," Vin's dad said. "Each one of us does the best we can."

"Is that some of your sage advice?" Vin teased.

His father shrugged. "What the heck. Sure. I've lived almost seventy years, and I've seen a lot. You know your mother and I only had you. We didn't have you until we were older, and everyone said she shouldn't have kids because of her age. But your mother got pregnant and was determined to have you. It was frightening for her, and I know that experience colored the way she parented."

"She was a tiger," Casey said. "I remember."

"Me too," Vin agreed and turned to his father. "Do you remember that time I was accused of stealing in class? I was in the third grade."

His dad nodded. "You said you didn't do it, and she believed you. I remember her marching down to that school and demanding that the teacher go through each of the desks. They didn't find anything, though. Then she asked the teacher if she had any proof. She didn't. She was just going on the fact that you had been sent back into the class to get something for her, and then the money was missing."

"Yup. I remember her raking my teacher over the coals while I sat outside in the hall. And she made her apologize to the entire class." Vin paused. "I didn't even know that the money was there. But I did know that my mom was going to stand up for me." Sometimes he missed her so much.

They entered the wooded area of the path. Brianna held back until they caught up to her, and she took Casey's hand. Apparently she didn't like the woods.

Then they crossed the spring run, and Brianna took off toward the play area once Casey said it was okay. "And they found the money the next day in the teacher's closet. She'd apparently forgotten that was where she'd put it. I'm surprised Mom didn't march down there again just to tell the teacher 'I told you so.'"

His dad chuckled. "She did at the next parent-teacher conference." He smiled as he watched Brianna run. "To have that much energy again," he said quietly as he continued in that direction. "I'm going to sit in the shade for a while." He wandered off, and Vin stayed with Casey, making their way to the play area.

Overlapping cries and shouts filled the air. It was a joyful cacophony as children ran, swung, slid, chased, and laughed. He loved that sound, and he leaned against the fence next to Casey, watching the goings-on. "Can I ask you something? Why did you become a police officer? At the funeral, you said you were going to go to business school."

"I was. But Alicia was having a baby, and I needed to have a paying job. And Dad had always expected me to join the force. Then Alicia left…." He shrugged and shook his head. "Everything in my life seemed to be changing all at once. I was really lucky things turned out so well. My mom and dad watch Brianna for me while I'm at work. That way I don't have to worry about finding someone who'll take her when I get odd shifts. I wouldn't be able to manage without their support."

"But you like being a cop," Vin said. It sure seemed like he did.

"Yeah. I get to help people, and I'm good at what I do." He grew quiet. "I keep going over in my mind what we know about the dealers who used your greenhouse. It's a small group, we believe. If there were too many, word would get out. But there is more than one group—that we know for sure. They don't put all their eggs in one basket."

"Okay. But what you took out of the greenhouse was small potatoes. In California, they plant acres in isolated and hard-to-reach areas. Why would they bother with such small plantings here? If it was me, I'd be looking for a place away from the road, in the country, where there was water nearby. I'd clear the area and plant. Then pump the water. It would be hard to spot the crops from the air with fields already cultivated nearby. You'd almost have to stumble on them that way." At least he thought so.

"We've gotten better at finding those sorts of things. The pictures from the air can now show us individual plants, they're so clear. It's the smaller places that are slipping through the cracks lately."

Vin nodded. "I see." He turned to Casey. "Then I'd look for what the places you *have* found have in common. They can't just be stumbling over them and putting plants there. Someone has to know about them and be familiar with what's going on." He caught Casey's gaze. "There has to be a way to en-sure that they aren't found right away and that they'll have access."

"You're right. There has to be some sort of con-nection between them all." Casey scratched his head. "But nothing stands out. I've looked at the locations we've come across so far, but they all seem so different. The only common denominator is that they are all out of the way and relatively easy to get to. Clients can get in and out without much effort."

"And maybe it's not even the locations themselves that we should be looking at. Maybe it's who might have access to each of them." Vin smiled slightly. "Take the shop. It's been there for years. But it would take someone who knew that it had been closed and that my father wasn't going over there on a regular basis to make it valuable. And since it's near the road, they would have to go in at night, when there's less traffic. And it's not like Dad would see it—it's the back of Dad's house, and the neighboring ones, that face the shop. I mean, it was a fluke that I saw the light. The neighbors are all very old and go to bed early. When you think about it, the greenhouse was a good site to use." He paused, his eyes widening. "I just had an idea. I'm going to ask the realtor for a list of showings. At least that would tell us the last time there was someone in there. The plants would have had to have been placed after that." When Casey nodded, Vin pulled out his phone and made a call.

"Jane, it's Vin Robins. I was wondering if you could do me a favor. We cleaned up the shop and the greenhouse like you suggested. Can you give me your email so I can send you some updated pictures?" The ones on the listing had been serviceable but not flattering.

"That would be great," she said brightly. "I'm anxious to get this property sold for your dad, and fresh pictures will help." She seemed to be a go-getter. Vin had liked her when he'd met her in the office a few days ago, while the police had the place under surveillance.

"I was thinking… you said you'd put together a list of all the showings so far, as well as the people who'd seemed interested. Would you mind if I took a look at it?" He turned to Casey, who seemed anxious. Vin's phone pinged with an email.

"I just sent it," Jane said. "Is there anything else?"

"No. I'm going to clean up the yard around the buildings before taking the pictures, but you'll have them tomorrow. Thank you for everything." He ended the call and checked out the email, then turned to Casey. "Where do you want me to send this?"

Casey offered his email address, and Vin forwarded the file. Once that was done, he opened it and peeked at the names and dates. "From this, it looks like the last showing was over five weeks ago."

Casey looked at the dates as well. "That means that the plants were brought in as seedlings. Someone would have had to water them regularly, but the greenhouse would have provided light and protection from wind. The last few weeks have been sunny, as I remember." He chewed his lower lip. "Thanks for this. It gives us a slightly clearer timeline. Judging by the report, there haven't been many showings. At least not lately."

"Nope. But then, our drug dealer friends would have to know that, and they were taking a chance that there wouldn't be another. They might even have a contact with the real estate agency. At this stage, anything's possible."

"Daddy, can I go feed the ducks?" Brianna asked, interrupting Vin's train of thought.

"Yes, but you have to ask Mr. Mack if he'll give you some corn," Casey told her. She rushed over to Vin's dad, who smiled and handed Brianna the entire bag. She skipped happily over toward the ducks as Vin walked beside Casey. He knew he couldn't take his hand, but they brushed a few times, and Casey smiled at him each and every time.

"Here, Daddy," she said, offering the bag to him and then Vin in turn. "Mr. Mack said I should share like he did." So they took turns feeding the ducks. "No, like this," she corrected Casey, tossing the corn as far as she could. The ducks all scrambled, and she giggled, then threw some more. Vin tossed a little corn but left most of it for Brianna, who was having a ball. Besides, Vin found Brianna's father a lot more interesting than the ducks. Vin couldn't seem to take his eyes off of Casey. His eyes and his smile were the same, but the boy Vin had known was gone. In his place, there was a strong, handsome man with broad shoulders and arms that pulled his shirtsleeves when he bent them. Young Casey had been good-looking, but this Casey was hot as hell.

"All right," Casey said once the corn was gone. "I think we should probably think about going home." Brianna whined a little, but Vin stopped her with a shake of his head.

"Frogs?" she asked a little gingerly, and Vin grinned.

"Okay. But we have to go back through the woods on the way. Are you ready to go?" She sure seemed to be, and their little group walked back the way they'd come, over the bridge and through the wooded area. They passed out into the open field and around the baseball diamond to the small creek. Only a trickle of water was running through the creek bed, but there was enough to create mud for the frogs.

"Where are they?"

Vin bent down, looking on either side the bank. "Look right there. See? It's just down there at the edge of the water."

She grinned. "Can you get it?" she asked in a stage whisper.

"That was how your dad and I fell in. I think it's best to leave the frogs alone so they can make more frogs." Vin loved this. It reminded him so much of when he and Casey used to come here back when they were kids. How many times had they come home soaking wet and covered in mud? At that thought, his imagination raced to imagining how Casey would look wet. He shivered a little in excitement but pushed that idea away. He didn't want to make a fool of himself in front of Casey and his daughter. "Shall we go?"

Brianna got up, then raced ahead. Vin got up as well, and Casey fell in with him, their hand brushing once again. "She never stops."

"Why don't you young people head on downtown? There's a car festival of some sort going on down there this weekend. I'm going to continue on home." Clearly his dad wanted a little peace and quiet… and probably a nap.

"Can we?" Brianna asked. "Will they have ice cream?" This kid had a hollow leg. She'd already been stuffed full of pizza.

"I don't know what they'll have, if anything. But, if it's okay with your daddy, it's okay with me," Vin told her.

She jumped in the air. "Yay." Obviously she was well aware that she had her daddy wrapped around her little finger.

"You have to be good and do what I tell you," Casey told her. She suddenly stopped running ahead of them and waited for them to catch up, then took Casey's hand. That had to be her "I'll be good" stance.

"I got lucky this weekend. Usually I have to work these festivals. The city likes to have the police department around. It usually staves off any trouble," Casey told him. "Not that there ever is any. These festivals are like the old town picnic. Everyone comes out and walks the closed-off streets to see what might be for sale, then they talk, get refreshments, and generally just have a good time. It doesn't seem to matter if it's Ford Week, Corvette Weekend, or a festival of the arts."

"I remember," Vin said. "It was just a chance for everyone to get out of the house and socialize with their neighbors." They turned at the corner and reached Hanover Street, the main north-south road through town. It was blocked off, with cars set up on either side. This weekend, there seemed to be some sort of antique car show, because there were classic vehicles of every description. Vin wasn't particularly interested, but Casey seemed to be, peering inside each one and explaining to Brianna why it was special.

"I see you still love these," Vin said gently. He remembered Casey working on his family's vehicles.

"Yeah. I have a '69 Mustang in the garage at my parents' place. I bought it years ago, and Dad and I worked on it for a while. We got the engine running well and are finishing up the body work. The upholstery is original and looks good, but the floors need work. I've been trying to find some carpet that I can use for them. There's still a lot of work to do, though." He shrugged. "Alicia hated that car. When I first brought it home, she insisted that I get rid of it. So I took it to Mom and Dad's place. Dad loves the car, but after he injured his back last year, he can't do a lot of the work any longer. And with Brianna…."

"There just isn't enough time," Vin finished for him.

Casey nodded. "And Brianna comes first. Always." A small carousel and a Ferris wheel had been set up on one of the side streets, and they let Brianna lead them over to them. She stayed with Vin while Casey got her tickets.

"Do you want me to go on the ride with you?" Casey asked.

Brianna looked at him like he was crazy. "No, Daddy. You can watch." She handed over her ticket and climbed up onto one of the lions, then held on and smiled brightly, waving until the ride slowly began to turn. Casey watched her, waving each time she came around.

Casey sighed. "When Alicia first left, Brianna asked me all the time if it was because Alicia didn't like her. I told her that Mommy wasn't happy with me, that it had nothing to do with her. And I promised myself that I'd do my very best for her."

Vin held the railing of the portable fencing around the ride, and Casey's hand rested partially on top of it.

Vin turned to where they touched and then looked up at Casey, who watched Brianna, waving again. "Casey… I…."

"I've missed you, Vin… for a long time. I didn't know who I was." His fingers closed slightly, and then he pulled away as the ride began to slow. "Back then, I had no idea about myself and I didn't know what I wanted. But things are different now."

Brianna climbed down and bounded over to where they waited. "That was fun." She peered up at both of them. "I'm ready for ice cream now."

"How about we finish looking at things here and then go home? I need to make dinner, and you can have ice cream for dessert. Okay?"

"But Daddy…." She pooched out that lower lip.

Vin had to give Casey credit—he didn't give in. Vin, on the other hand, was ready to fold like a house of cards, already on the verge of pulling out his wallet.

"We have your favorite ice cream at home—it's chocolate. And you can add sprinkles and whipped cream if you'd like. But it's getting late. If you eat ice cream now, you won't eat your dinner."

When she started to sulk, he added, "You know that isn't going to do you any good. And if you keep it up, you'll go to bed right after dinner. And there won't be dessert." He was firm, and she quieted. After five minutes, though, she was back to being her usual adorable self, and they wandered around the area for another half an hour or so.

"Is Mr. Vin going to have dinner with us?" Brianna asked.

"I should check on my dad," Vin said, not wanting to intrude.

"Mr. Vin," Brianna said, taking his hand, "Daddy cooks good. I promise."

"Come to dinner," Casey said, and Vin found himself agreeing. It would be best if he just went back to his dad's place and let this go. It was an old crush, and he was over it. Casey was his friend— *only* his friend. And he was going back to California in a matter of days. Unfortunately, the mere touch of Casey's hand on his had him wishing for things he'd long known were out of the question.

"Yay. When we get home, I can show you all my Barbies and where they live. I have lots of them, and each one is different. Only Malibu Barbie gets to live in the house." She babbled on, telling him more than he wanted to know about each doll.

Vin met Casey's gaze quizzically.

"Brianna, it's okay. Mr. Vin doesn't need to know the personal history of each one of your Barbies. And he's coming to dinner, not taking up residence. Okay?" He was so gentle.

"Okay, Daddy," she said. "Can I can help make you dinner?"

Was this what it was like to have a child? Brianna could be such a little girl at times, but then she'd turn around and do or say something that made her seem so much older. And it was obvious that she considered it her job to look after her father. Casey was a very lucky man.

CASEY LIVED near downtown, in one of the mid-Victorian-era row homes. It was little more than a room wide, but four rooms deep, and seemed a bit like a construction zone. "I'm working on the floors one room at a time, and I still need to put the furniture back in place. I just finished one yesterday, so the front room resembles a warehouse at the moment." Casey led him to the very back of the house, where a lovely three-season room opened to a simple backyard. "I'm not sure what I'm going to do out there yet."

"The floors are lovely." The rooms looked like they'd all been cleaned up with fresh paint and deep, dark woodwork. "This must have been a lot of work."

Casey nodded. "Yeah, but I love it. Unfortunately, everything is a bit of a tangle right now. Alicia is pushing me to sell it because she wants the money. But there is nothing for her to get. With the real estate crunch of a few years ago, we're no longer under water, but the mortgage is just about what the house is worth. I've been paying it for the last couple of years."

"Are you in the process of getting a divorce?" Vin asked, wishing he could help somehow.

"Yes. It's complicated, though, because she refuses to return. Not only is that hurting her case, but it's also hurting her daughter." He stood gripping the back of the chair in front of him. "I just don't know how to make it up to Brianna. I've tried to get Alicia to understand that by leaving and staying away, she's only making it harder on herself." Casey's knuckles were turning white, he was gripping the chair so hard. "I've had people shoot at me, and I can keep a cool head under pressure. But when it comes to what that woman's doing to Brianna…."

"Your daughter is your heart," Vin said for him, and Casey nodded.

"Alicia keeps insisting that Brianna come down to Costa Rica to live with her, but that will never happen." Casey went to a small desk in the corner. He opened a drawer and pulled out some papers. When Casey handed them to Vin, he looked them over.

"Jesus," he breathed. "She really sent these?"

Casey nodded. "Yes. The original emails and notes are with my attorney. But basically she says that I'm sick—because I'm gay—and that it's not safe for Brianna to be with me. But if you think this one is bad, read the second one. That's where she threatens to take Brianna away from me, saying she'll make sure I never see her again. She actually says that Costa Rica is the only place that Brianna will be safe from the likes of me." Vin read the pages over and handed them back.

At first he didn't understand why Casey was showing him all of this, and then it hit him. Casey was falling into the old patterns that had been ingrained after years of friendship. As kids they had shared almost all their secrets. As far as he knew, Vin was the only person who knew that Casey had once stolen a video game from the store in town. Only they'd both felt so guilty about it, neither one of them had been able to play the game. The next week, they had gone into the store, and while Vin kept the clerk occupied, Casey had put the game back.

"Do you think any judge is going to allow her any sort of custody of Brianna?" Vin asked.

Casey shrugged. "I don't know. I hope not. Alicia is trying to sue down there, as well as here, but I don't think she's going to get very far. We were married here, and Brianna lives here—we all did. So in essence, she's walked away from Brianna. So I think I'm safe as far as custody is concerned. But what I'm afraid of is this. What if a court here grants her some sort of unsupervised visitation? And the first time she takes Brianna, Alicia spirits her away to Costa Rica? If that happens, I'll never see my daughter again."

Vin didn't know what to say. He wanted to tell Casey that Alicia couldn't possibly steal Brianna away from him. But he knew the vagaries of the law well enough to know that Casey's fear was warranted.

"Not that I have any intention of letting Brianna go down there for any reason," Casey continued. "I intend to keep her safe. And if Alicia wants to visit, then I'd gladly let her see Brianna—under supervision, of course. A little girl needs her mother." He seemed heartbroken.

"I think…." Vin swallowed. "I think that a little girl—or a little boy, for that matter—just needs a parent who loves them and puts them first. I'm sure Brianna asks about her mother now and then, but she knows it's you who's here every day for her. And that's what counts."

"Daddy," Brianna said as she ran into the room. "Is dinner ready?"

He scooped her up. "Sorry, sweetheart. I haven't started it yet."

"I'll help you with it after I put my toys away," she said, then raced away.

Vin could only smile. That kid was something else. "I can help too," he offered.

A few minutes later, they were all in the kitchen, making dinner together. At first glance, they looked like the perfect family.

If only....

CHAPTER 4

EVERYONE SEEMED to enjoy dinner, and once Casey got Brianna settled at the table with her bowl of chocolate ice cream, complete with sprinkles *and* whipped cream, he excused himself to take care of the dishes. He had just finished up when the doorbell sounded. Casey wiped his hands and went to answer it… and was immediately sorry he had.

"What are you doing here?" Speak of the devil. Damn, he'd just been talking about her. Maybe he should have learned something from *Beetlejuice*.

"I came to see my daughter," Alicia snapped. "I'd have thought that would be obvious." She tried to push past him, but Casey wasn't having it.

"That's very nice. But you could have called to let me know."

She tried to push in again. "Brianna is my daughter. I have a right to see her. This is my house too, and—"

Casey held his ground. He had always wondered how he'd react at this moment, and now it was here. "First, this house is not yours. Because you never attended any of the court proceedings, it was awarded to me. All that's left is the final divorce decree. And secondly, you can see Brianna, but not tonight. It's late, and I'm not letting anyone—including you—force their way into the house to upset her." He ran his hand through his hair and took a deep breath. "Look, you can join us for lunch tomorrow if you want." Everything inside his head told him to keep calm and stay in control of the situation. He turned as Vin peered around the corner. He caught his eye and hoped he managed to convey the message to keep Brianna away.

"I want to see *my* daughter," Alicia persisted.

Vin disappeared, hopefully taking Brianna to the back of the house, because Alicia was starting to get adamant.

"And you will. Tomorrow, at lunch." He pushed her outside, then walked out too, closing the door behind them. "I'm sorry, but you've been gone for nearly two years. You can't just barge in because you blew into town."

He wasn't having this. All that mattered was his daughter. "Brianna asks about you. It will be good for the two of you to talk. So come by tomorrow and you'll get your chance."

She set her jaw, but Casey was ready for the fight. When he'd first met Alicia, he'd thought she was kind and caring. Once they were married, though, he'd discovered it was all an act. Alicia was caring, all right—she cared about herself, first and foremost. And the longer they were together, the more unreasonable her demands became. Once he figured himself out enough to tell her that he was attracted to men as well as women, she had become impossible to live with. Not that they had ever had a great marriage. When Brianna was six months old, she'd declared that she didn't want a *maricón* for a husband. The last time she'd seen Brianna was two years ago.

After Alicia left, guilt had taken hold of Casey in a large way. He knew he had hurt Alicia by using her to try to get past his feelings for Vin. That hadn't been fair to her. But he had done his best to be a good husband, and he'd been faithful to her and to their marriage.

He had a feeling that some of that guilt still lingered. Brianna's birth had been difficult and had taken a great deal out of Alicia. The doctors had said that she might not be able to have more children. Casey wondered if that was why she had decided to show up now.

"Do you have a man in there? Is that what's going on? You and some guy are cavorting around while my daughter is right there?" She began to shake.

Casey put his arms over his chest. "Why are you here? It's been years since you bothered with

Brianna. Why now?" He pinned Alicia with his gaze, and she glared back at him.

Alicia broke first, and for a second he saw a glimpse of the person he thought he knew. "I've found someone else. He would be a much better father to Brianna than a *maricón* like you."

So he'd been right. Now that Alicia had someone new in her life, she wanted Brianna to round out her little family.

"Stop it," Casey snapped. "That's Vin. He and I have been friends since we were in school together. And I'm not going to stand here and let you badmouth my friends. You were the one who walked out. Don't forget that." He sighed. "You know, maybe I should check with my lawyer before I let you see Brianna. Of course, that could take days…." He glared at her, and some of the heat in her gaze cooled. Regardless of how he felt about her, she was Brianna's mother, and Casey was trying to be decent. But apparently no good deed went unpunished around Alicia. "Come by tomorrow at noon. I'm sure Brianna will be happy to see you."

Her shoulders slumped slightly, and she nodded. "All right." She finally turned, then walked down the sidewalk to a Mercedes and got in the passenger seat. Casey noted the license plate as it pulled away, and then went back inside.

"Was that Alicia?" Vin asked.

"Yeah. She tried to muscle her way in to see Brianna. She's going to drop by for lunch with her tomorrow." Alicia was always one to push and push. It was her way of getting what she wanted. The only way he had found of countering it was to wait her out. He shook his head. "I don't think I'm being un-reasonable. Brianna has no idea that she's here, and I want to be the one to tell her about Alicia." Now that his ex was gone, Casey wondered how long it was going to take for him to let go of the damn guilt. But really, would it have killed her to make a simple phone call and let him know she was on her way? Was that too much to ask?

"Look, I should go. You've got your hands full, first talking to Brianna, then trying to get her into bed." Vin smiled. "It's been amazing getting to see you again, and…." He rocked slightly from foot to foot. "I've missed you. I'm glad you told me how you feel."

Casey stilled. "I don't think I've…."

Vin drew closer, the heat off his body setting Casey's heart beating faster. "There are lots of ways to tell someone that you care for them. And not all of them require words." He closed the distance be-tween them and took Casey's hand. Fire radiated up Casey's arm, blooming all over him. His mouth went dry, and all that mattered was that Vin didn't stop.

"Vin," he whispered, aware that Brianna was in the back room. He stilled when Vin closed the small gap between them until they were almost touching. Then he paused, and Casey waited a second, wonder-ing what Vin was doing. Then he took the leap, mov-ing the final distance until their lips touched. Vin tast-ed of spice and warmth. For the longest time, Casey had wondered what kissing Vin would be like. Even his teenage fantasies hadn't lived up to the reality.

"Daddy!" Brianna called, and Vin stepped back, breathing hard, his eyes wide.

"Hey, sweetheart," Casey forced himself to say as he reluctantly looked away from Vin. "Are you done with your dessert?"

She nodded. "And I showed Mr. Vin some of my Barbies. But not the ones with the house. Those are all upstairs getting ready for bed."

"And you should do the same." He picked her up and hugged her tightly. "Go brush your teeth and wash your hands and face. Then get into bed and I'll come up to tuck you in." He set her down.

"Okay." Brianna turned to Vin and held up her arms. Vin lifted her, and Brianna gave him a hug. "Thank you for coming to feed the ducks with us." She patted him on the shoulder, and Vin lowered her back to her feet. Then she climbed the stairs as Casey saw Vin to the door.

"Are you going to be okay tomorrow?" Vin asked. "Should you have someone else here while she visits?"

"I'll call my lawyer in the morning and let her know what's going on. Heather is a smart cookie. She'll let me know if there's anything I should be on the lookout for. She may want to come over herself. I'm not sure." Casey lightly scratched the back of his head, more out of nerves than anything else. "Besides, I'm afraid that if I have someone here, no matter who that person is, Alicia is going to accuse me of some sort of impropriety."

Vin nodded slowly. "I heard part of her little tirade before you got her outside. I don't think Brianna did, though. She didn't seem to know that Alicia was even here."

"Good, thank you. I'll tell her what's going on when I go upstairs." Hopefully it would be okay. But after all this time, Casey didn't know how Brianna would react to the news.

"Call me if you need me." Vin placed his hands on each of Casey's cheeks, warming his face before kissing him again. This time his lips lingered, but the touch remained gentle. Casey wanted to pull Vin to him and feast on his plump lips, but before his mind caught up, Vin had pulled back. "I have to say good night now, because if I don't…." Vin's voice was rough and deep, and his eyes darkened as he turned and opened the door. "Talk to you tomorrow." Then he left, leaving Casey with only the lingering scent of him in the air. He inhaled deeply, trying to catch a last whiff of him before it dissipated. Sometimes Casey thought that he had to worst timing on earth.

He reminded himself yet again that he needed to keep his mind and his heart where they belonged— on his daughter. Brianna needed his attention, and he couldn't allow his feelings for Vin to get him muddled and confused. Vin was leaving, and no matter how good a kisser he was—or what dreams those two soft kisses had ignited—Casey had to keep his feet firmly planted on the ground and his heart under control.

THE NEXT day, Casey put together a list of everything they'd come across on the series of drug finds, culminating with the one at the greenhouse at

Mack's. "Find anything new?" Carter asked as he stopped at his desk.

"I wish. I know there's something that I'm missing, but I can't put my finger on it. This scattered model they're using is…." Casey sighed and checked his watch.

"Got a hot date?" Carter asked with a teasing grin.

"I wish." He thought of Vin and wished that he was the person Casey would be seeing in a couple of hours, instead of his ex-wife. Just thinking about him made the temperature in the room rise a few degrees. But somehow, knowing he had Vin in his life again made the coming ordeal with Alicia a little easier to bear. He knew that ultimately Alicia just wanted Brianna. And that wasn't going to happen. He only wished she'd realize that and back off. But that wasn't Alicia's style. She preferred the "wear you down until you give in" approach. "I'm seeing my ex-wife."

"I'm sorry, man." He leaned over his desk.

"Me too. I'd much rather be out with Vin." He met Carter's gaze, half expecting some kind of censure.

"The guy from the greenhouse?" Carter met his gaze when he nodded. "You guys have been friends forever, right?"

"Yeah, and I guess you never really forget your first love." As soon as the words were out of his mouth, he wished he could take them back. He and Carter really didn't have that kind of friendship. In fact, they'd been little more than colleagues up until now, though that was probably Casey's fault. The other officers were close to each other, but Casey always felt like he was on the outside looking in.

"That's pretty cool. So are the two of you getting back together?" Carter seemed a little like an excited puppy. Maybe all Casey needed to do was open up more often.

"I don't know." He swallowed hard. "I think I'd like to. Losing him was that one big regret. But now I have Brianna, and…." Casey let his voice trail off.

"So? Donald and I have Alex, and it wasn't all roses for us." Carter clapped him hard on the shoulder. "If you don't go for what you want, you'll never get it."

Casey knew that was true. "Speaking of going for it, are you taking the lieutenant's exam?" He had heard Carter talking about it in the locker room a few times.

"I'm thinking about it."

"Then take your own advice," Casey told him.

Carter nodded and they returned to their review of what they'd found on the drug ring, but they didn't really make any headway before it was time for Casey to leave.

CASEY REFUSED to be nervous. Even though Vin wasn't there, Casey knew his friend was only a phone call away if he needed him. That gave Casey the strength he'd need to get through the next few hours. Alicia was going to be there soon. He'd made his chicken salad, the kind that he knew Alicia liked, with a touch of curry, pineapple, and nuts. When he'd stumbled on the recipe, she had adored it, so he used to make it quite often.

"Is Mommy mad at me?" Brianna asked. It was the third time she'd questioned him since he'd told her that Alicia was coming to lunch.

"No, sweetheart," he reassured her. "If anything, she's mad at me. Not you."

"Why?" Brianna sat in one of the chairs, her beautiful eyes staring at him. "Why don't you and Mommy just say sorry and then she can come back here to live?" It seemed like the perfect solution for a six-year-old.

"Because your mommy and I don't love each other like we used to. She wants to live in Costa Rica, and you and I live here. I still love your mommy, but not in a way that she and I can still be married." If she had come back shortly after leaving, he'd have taken her back for Brianna's sake. But now that she'd been away for two years with almost no communication between them, that was out of the question.

"But why?" Brianna asked.

Here was where the truth got much more complicated. Casey leaned against the counter, clutching the edge behind him. "Because we don't feel that way anymore. But that doesn't mean that we don't love you. We do."

"Is that because you love boys instead of girls now?" Brianna asked.

Casey's breath caught in his throat. Then he took a deep breath. "Where did you hear that?" he asked as calmly as he could. He and Brianna hadn't talked about that yet.

"Grandma said it to Grandpa when they didn't think I could hear."

Casey needed to remember that his daughter had batlike hearing. Very little escaped her. "Well, yes. I think I like boys," he agreed.

"Does that mean you wish I was a boy?" Tears were already forming, and Casey lifted her up.

"Nope. You're my best girl, and I love you more than anything. I'm happy you are just who you are, because that makes you perfect. What it means is that I think the next time I get married, I will marry a boy instead of a girl. Okay?" Inside, he pleaded with the universe that she'd let the topic drop. No such luck.

"Like Mr. Vin?" she asked, and just like that his thoughts went to the man he had been telling himself he needed to stop thinking about. "I like him, Daddy. And if you want to marry Mr. Vin, then it's okay with me." She giggled and her arms went around his neck, holding him tight. Sometimes he wondered who was the parent in this family.

"How about we put this talk of Daddy marrying boys aside. It might hurt Mommy's feelings." God, he so did not want to be having this conversation with Alicia arriving in half an hour. He just need-ed this visit to be over with quickly, without a huge fight. He was determined not to let her get to him.

"Okay. No talking about that." She pulled back until he looked in her eyes.

"I love you, sweetheart, and I always will. No matter what, I'm your daddy, and I will love you for always, forever and ever." He hugged her tight again so Brianna didn't see the tears that filled his eyes. He could talk someone down from jumping from a roof and remain calm, he'd stared down a man with a gun pointed right at him and stayed cool, but if his little girl was upset, then he went to pieces. She was the only person in his life that he was not going to lose, no matter what.

"I love you, Daddy, bestest and mostest." She hugged him again, and Casey set her down.

"Why don't you go upstairs and get dressed. You want to look nice for Mommy, right?" As she hurried up the stairs, Casey took a few seconds to calm his breath and get himself under control before he followed her. Once she was dressed, they went back downstairs, and Brianna helped him put things out on the table.

His phone vibrated, and he hoped to hell it was some emergency at work. At least he'd have an excuse to call this whole thing off. Instead it was a message from Vin. *Is everything okay? Do you want a get-out-of-jail-free call?* Casey couldn't help smiling.

Yeah. At one o'clock. Thanks. Damn, Vin was amazing to have thought of that, and Casey was grateful to the fates or whatever cosmic force had brought Vin back into his life, even if it was for only a short time. Casey hadn't realized how much he'd missed his friend and how empty parts of his heart had been until he'd found Vin again. He sent the message and got a smiley face with devil horns in return as a firm knock sounded out front. Casey took his phone off vibrate and slipped it in his pocket, then took Brianna's hand, figuring they'd answer it together.

Alicia stood out front. A man Casey didn't know stood at the bottom of the steps, behind her. The Mercedes he'd seen the night before was parked

across the street. "Mija," she said as she stepped toward Brianna, who shifted behind Casey to hide.

"Hello, Alicia," he said gently. "Come inside."
He turned his attention to the man, who stayed where
he was. "Can I help you?"

"This is Renaldo," she said with a warm smile.
Casey had once seen that smile flashed in his direction
and knew how potent it could be. She extended her
hand to her "friend," and he came up the stairs to take
it. Lord, it seemed that Alicia had decided to bring her
smarmy boyfriend along with her. Casey noticed how
his hard gaze didn't seem to settle anywhere. It was a
little unsettling, but he had almost no time to think on
it as his mind careened back to what was important.

"Alicia, this visit was so you could see Brianna,"
Casey told her firmly. He turned to the man. "There
are some wonderful shops downtown. You might
want to check out a few of them." The man released
Alicia's hand and said something to her in rapid Span-
ish. They talked briefly, and then Renaldo turned and
went stiffly to the car. Casey half expected him to protest. Only once the car door had closed behind him did
Casey step back and invite Alicia inside.

"I can see your manners have deteriorated since
I left," she commented with only a hint of her accent.

Casey closed the door. "My manners are just
fine," he said gently, but met her gaze with a steely
one of his own. She could try playing games, but it
wasn't going to work. Brianna stayed close to him,
and Casey lifted her into his arms. She was almost
too big to lift, but when she was worried, she still
wanted her daddy.

"Mija," Alicia said to her.

"Hi, Mommy," Brianna said, still holding on to him. It was like they were almost strangers. Casey gave her a hug and then set Brianna back down.

"Why don't you take your mommy into the kitchen? You can tell her all about your dolls, and I'll get lunch ready." Alicia held out her hand, but Brianna hurried ahead. Alicia was clearly disappointed, but she kept her comments to herself.

"This is the Barbie I play with," Brianna said. "Her name is Daphne, and she's really smart." Brianna climbed into her chair and handed the doll to Alicia, who looked at it briefly, then set it aside. Brianna took the doll back and held her.

"I came especially to see you," Alicia said.

Brianna nodded but said very little. This visit wasn't going well, as far as Casey could see. Brianna didn't know what to say to Alicia, and it seemed to him that Alicia had expected Brianna to cry and miss her terribly.

"That's nice. Did you come from Costa… Rico?"

"Costa Rica, yes. That's where your abuela and abuelo live. My entire family is there, and they'd very much like to meet you." She smiled. "Would you like to come visit?"

Brianna turned to him. "Daddy, can we go there?"

"I meant just you and me," Alicia said. "I could get plane tickets for us, and we could go visit and you could meet everybody. They'd love you, and—"

"That's enough, Alicia. You may visit Brianna here. I'm sure she'd like to see you. But she isn't going to Costa Rica with you." He remained calm—barely—even as he seethed on the inside. Casey made up a plate for Brianna and put it in front of her with a glass of milk and flatware.

"Sweetheart, your mom and I need to talk." He motioned to the other room, and Alicia heaved a sigh before getting up. He wasn't sure she'd do as he asked. But she did.

"I'd like to take my daughter to see *my* family. Is that too much to ask?" Alicia argued as soon as they left the room.

Casey closed the door to the kitchen. "Here are the facts, Alicia. You left two years ago. We are officially separated with only the official divorce decree outstanding, and since you abandoned her, the courts have granted me full custody. Brianna isn't going anywhere with you—certainly not out of the country. I'm very happy that you've visited. She deserves to know her mother. But that's it. You can either have a nice lunch with her and spend some time, or you can leave. Either way, it's your decision. And what you talk about will be noted, and a letter will be sent to my lawyer. I always thought you were a good mother… up until you simply left her." He softened his tone and expression as best he could. "Be that good mother now. Okay? Just rebuild your relationship with Brianna."

She gasped in shock, eyes wide. "I *am* her mother."

"A mother she hasn't seen in two years," Casey reiterated. "There is very little relationship left. She asks me if you hate her and if you left because of her." He could tell Alicia was gearing up for an argument just by her posture. "It doesn't matter why you left. I know it wasn't because of her, and I've told her that. But you need to show her that you really care. And you aren't going to do that by fighting with me or being petty."

"You said that to her?" Alicia asked. "That I didn't leave because of her?"

"Of course I did. I told you I wanted you to visit. That I want you and Brianna to have a relationship. Just know that she will not be leaving the country. That isn't going to happen."

"I was thinking that maybe both of you could come down…."

Casey shook his head. "No. I'm not taking her to Costa Rica, where your family has influence." He narrowed his gaze. "Some things are facts, and they won't change. But I also won't stop you from seeing Brianna." He peered out the door and then opened it. "Go spend time with her."

Alicia nodded and joined Brianna at the table. Casey made up a plate for her and offered it to Alicia. Then he took his plate into the next room. He could see the two of them, but it would give them some time to talk. Casey had finished his lunch when his phone rang. It was Vin.

"How is it going?" he asked.

"Yes. I can work that schedule," Casey answered.

"I see. They can hear you and you want Alicia to think it's work. Okay. I can do that. Do you want me to call you later?"

"No, I can be there in an hour to take care of that. I'll need to bring my daughter, but it shouldn't take very long." He figured Vin would pick up on the message.

"Okay. I'll call in half an hour to remind you that you're needed. But I need you to come here. I think someone has been back in the greenhouse. Maybe you can take a look."

"No problem. I'll take care of it," Casey said and ended the call. He put his phone back in his pocket, knowing Alicia had been listening to every word. "Would either of you like some more?" He took his plate to the sink. Alicia and Brianna were talking, with his daughter telling her mother about school and all her friends.

"Thank you," Alicia said as she handed him her plate. "That was always a favorite."

"That's why I made it," he said softly. Casey didn't hate Alicia. He found it impossible to hate the mother of the child he adored most in this world.

She checked her watch and stood. "I know you have an appointment, and Renaldo is going to be back to pick me up." She stood and gathered her things. "Can I see you again?" she asked Brianna, and Casey nodded when she looked at him.

"How long will you be here?"

"A few more days. I work as an interior decorator in Costa Rica, and this is a busy time of year for me. Renaldo has business here, but he needs to return soon as well." She knelt down, and Brianna gave her mother a hug but then backed right away and went to Casey for reassurance. He took her hand, and they showed Alicia to the door. At that moment, Renaldo pulled up in front of the house. Alicia got in the car, and then they drove away.

Casey closed the door, wondering what Alicia was up to. It wasn't like her to capitulate so easily, especially after getting herself so worked up over something she thought was her right. Alicia was many things, but she didn't shy away from a fight. He was pretty sure that today was a strategic retreat and nothing more. "Do we have to go somewhere?"

"Yes. Mr. Vin needs to see me, and I thought that we could go visit Mr. Mack, if that's okay with you. I was thinking we could stop at the bakery and bring cupcakes," he said conspiratorially. Brianna obviously liked that idea—she was all grins. Casey took care of the dishes and then got them ready to go.

"IT WASN'T like this before," Vin said as Casey knelt to examine the pane of glass. It hadn't been broken but had been placed on the ground, on the wooded side of the long, rectangular greenhouse. The empty space left by missing pane was just off the ground at the foundation of the greenhouse structure. The walls went up another six feet or so before the roof sloped to a peak.

"I believe you're right. But why not just break the glass to get in?" Casey asked.

"It's not that simple. This is reinforced glass so it can withstand the weather. Breaking it would make plenty of noise, where working it loose would be quiet. What I don't understand is what they were looking for." Vin stayed where he was while Casey took a look around. He'd checked everything over and hadn't found anything. The inside was remarkably clean.

"Maybe they lost something and came back to see if it's still here? Something small, maybe, that we might have missed when we confiscated the plants and drugs." Casey checked over the area where the plants and the labeled bins had been. "Get a rake. The metal kind for gardening, please. Let's turn over the ground and see if we can find something." It was probably a futile effort, but it couldn't hurt to be thorough. Vin left the greenhouse, then returned from the back of the shop with a rake.

"What can I do to help?" Vin asked as Casey got to work, systematically turning the ground around where the plants had been.

"In the glove compartment of my car are evidence bags. Could you get a couple in case they're needed?" He continued working, carefully digging up the area, but only came up with more compacted dirt.

"Anything?" Vin asked when he returned.

Casey shook his head. "Not yet." He continued raking slowly. "Was there anything missing from the shop?"

"No. That's the strange thing. I don't even think they went in there. No dirt was tracked inside, and nothing was disturbed at all. Whatever they were looking for seems to have been out here." Vin's nerves were obvious. "I just wish these people would just leave things alone. Dad had a showing yesterday, and the couple seemed really interested. He works in Harrisburg, and they're just moving to the area. I don't know if anything will come of it, but it isn't going to happen if someone's breaking in all the time."

Casey slowly worked the rake into the top layer of soil, paying special attention to those areas that were loose. The hardpack wasn't going to conceal anything.

A glint of metal caught the light, and he paused to remove an old bottle top. Still, he put it in one of the evidence bags and marked it, though he was pretty sure it had been there for quite some time. Still, he kept going, working from the very back toward the shop.

"What's this?" Vin asked, peering around the leg of one of the plant racks. "A key."

"Don't touch it," Casey told him and grabbed a bag. He used that to pick up the fob and key from the ground. It was worn and had a BMW logo on it. The car it fit was likely an older model. It had the ability to lock and unlock the car, but it also contained a standard key, so tracing it was going to be difficult. Well, tracing almost any key to the car it belonged to was a shot in the dark. "At least it tells us the kind of car we're looking for."

"Unless it's been dumped already." Vin peered at the key. "They came back and didn't find it, so they'll want to kill the trail. You've said these guys are smart enough to keep ahead of you. They aren't going to keep using this car, even if they have the second key." What Vin said made sense, but Casey called it in anyway, adding details to his report and putting out a BOLO. They might get lucky if they acted quickly.

"Let's see if there's anything else," Casey suggested, and they checked everywhere, with Casey raking the rest of the loose areas. They found nothing else. Casey wiped his brow with the back of his hand.

Vin chuckled. "All you did was smear the dirt," he said and went into the shop. He returned with an old damp towel. Casey held still as Vin wiped his forehead, the movements gentle. Casey closed his eyes at first but opened them again when Vin finished and set the towel aside. "I thought of you last night."

Casey swallowed. "You did?"

Vin nodded. "I kept thinking about this." He closed the distance and kissed him. Their last few kisses had been soft, but this time, Vin deepened it, sliding his warm hand around the back of Casey's neck, holding him still. Vin didn't apply any pressure, just pressed closer, his hand adding heat and warmth that spread through Casey like wildfire. In seconds, his pants grew uncomfortably tight, and he moaned softly into the kiss, taking more of what Vin had to offer.

"I'm sorry," Vin said when he pulled away. "I probably shouldn't be doing this. We're friends, and I have to go back to California, and…." His words came between panting breaths. "But damn, I've wanted you for years, and now you're right here. Maybe we just need to get each other out of our systems so we can move on. I don't know…." Vin hesitated and then placed his hands on Casey's shoulders, looking deep enough into his eyes that Casey felt the gaze like a touch to his soul. "Would it be wrong to say that I've been in love with you in some way since I was sixteen years old?" He sighed. "Sometimes my timing just sucks."

Casey lightly held Vin's arms, desire and pure need settling deep inside. He wanted Vin so badly he could taste it. Hell, he wanted to taste *him*, but he held himself back. "I know how you feel. The timing in my life seems all wrong too. And yet somehow, we were given this week." He took a deep breath, inhaling Vin's intoxicating scent, which nearly stripped away his control. He knew that no matter what happened, at the end when Vin left, it was going to hurt. "Maybe this is all the time we're supposed to have. I know it sounds stupid, but maybe we're supposed to make the most of this time because this is all we're going to get." He squeezed Vin's arm. "I don't know."

"I don't either," Vin whispered and let his hands fall to his side. "The easy thing to do would be to just walk away. You could go about your life, and I'd go home to Los Angeles next weekend…." Vin's words hung in the air. Casey had to agree that what Vin said was right. It would be safer for both of them if they just stayed friends.

"You're right, of course." He took a deep breath and stepped back. It didn't take a rocket scientist to see that getting involved, no matter what his heart urged him to do, would be a mistake. "It would be best if you and I just stayed friends. Lord knows it would be so much easier for both of us." He should just turn and leave. That would be the smart thing to do. Yet he stood still, his legs refusing the commands his mind was sending.

"Yeah. I should go check on Dad…." Vin didn't move either. His gaze stayed on Casey, like an invisible hand holding him in place. Casey knew that if Vin looked away, the spell would be broken, and it would be easy for Casey to leave. But he couldn't, not with Vin looking at him with those beautiful blue eyes flecked with a touch of green. Casey swallowed, and Vin did the same. It was like a game of mirror, and they each held the other spellbound.

If a car had backfired or if Brianna had come out, the moment would have been over. Whatever it was between him and Vin seemed held together by a spider's thread. Casey had no idea what was going to happen until Vin inched closer. Then he knew what Vin really wanted. There were no words, no spoken agreement, just Casey's heart relaxing, telling him this was what it wanted as well. He leaned closer, and then he was in Vin's arms, being kissed to within an inch of his life.

Vin quivered, and Casey closed his arms around him, holding him in return, pressing their bodies together. Excitement built until Vin backed away. Casey blinked and wondered what had happened until Vin took his hand and led him out of the greenhouse and into the shop. There, Vin practically spun him into his arms once again and held him tightly. Their kiss turned volcanic, and Casey pressed Vin back against the table, lifting him off his feet.

He was on fire, and his cock ached to be released. Lust and passion were quickly taking over all reason and caution. His heart pounded in his ears, and Vin's scent grew heady, driving him forward. But some semblance of rational thought still existed, and for a few seconds he looked away, realizing where they were. That alone held him back, and he turned to Vin, forcing his instinct down as he backed away.

"What?" Vin asked breathily.

"No. Not here," Casey said softly. "I'm not going to take you on the table out here like we're doing something wrong and have to hide. I won't do that." He took a huge breath, calming the raging hormones that threatened the control of reason. "I can't. Not like you're some secret I need to keep."

Vin nodded. "I…."

Casey swallowed hard, almost unable to believe he was saying this. "I spent my life hiding who I was. I know now, and I'm going to live my life in the open." He was aware that Alicia would do her best to use whatever decisions he made in his life to try to hurt him, one way or another. But in two years, he had come a long way in figuring things out. "If you and I are going to be intimate, then it will be in a proper bed where we can take our time."

Vin's eyebrows rose to his hairline as he climbed down. "Yeah…." He blinked and seemed to bring himself back to the present. "You're right."

"Come to dinner tonight. I'll cook, and once Brianna is in bed and asleep, then you and I can see what happens." Vin was worth more to him than a quick fuck on a table in a closed florist shop. If they only had so much time, then Casey was going to make sure that they made the most of it. Still, it took a while for his body to catch up with his head. "For now, I think it's best if I get Brianna and drop this off at the station." Maybe Carter and his computers could find out something about it.

"Okay. I'll see you at dinner. What time do you want me?" Damn, the wicked glint in Vin's eyes was enticing.

CHAPTER 5

"I'VE GOT dinner ready for you, Dad," Vin said as he tucked in his shirt. He found his father in the family room, sitting in front of the television.

"Will you be home tonight?" he asked, sitting forward.

That was extremely direct, especially for his father. Vin shrugged. "I don't know." He approached his father's chair. "Does that bother you?"

Dad chuckled slightly. "No. It doesn't bother me in the least. I like Casey. As kids, the two of you were hell on wheels. But you've both grown into good men." He sat back. "I met your mother in school. She and I dated for a while, and it didn't work out. I met her again years later. She was taking care of your grandmother, and this time when I saw her, it was like fireworks. I was nearly thirty and thought I'd be a bachelor for the rest of my life. But I knew that first time I saw her again that she was the one for me. She always had been, but I was too stupid to know the first time."

Vin sat in the other chair. "Did you cheat on Mom or something?" he asked, but his father shrugged. "What happened?"

"I thought Wendy Carmichael was the one for me. So when I got the chance, I took her out. She was nice but boring as all get-out. I had one date with her, but it cost me ten years without your mother. It was a huge price to pay, and I always regretted it. Sometimes in life, we only get one shot. But other times, if we're lucky as hell, we get a second chance." His dad shifted, and his intense gaze focused on Vin. "Rarely do we get a third chance at anything." Then he sat back and returned his attention to the game show on television.

Vin stood up and grabbed his keys, then left the house. He decided to walk to Casey's. It was a wonderful night with the early summer flowers in bloom. Carlisle had always been incredibly walkable, and he loved the fresh air. It seemed a number of others had the same idea, and Vin smiled at people as they passed him. He remembered these streets when he was a kid. A lot had changed—a large number of older buildings had recently been renovated, for one thing—but basically the town was the same. Businesses changed, but others were still there, and the town still felt like the same small town he'd grown up in. It was good to be home again.

When he reached the corner, Vin turned left onto Pomfret and continued on for a block and a half until he got to Casey's door. He passed a Mercedes, then saw Alicia descend Casey's stairs, the smile she'd been wearing sliding into a scowl as she yanked open the door of the car and got inside. He continued past the car and on down the sidewalk until the gray Mercedes sped off down the road. Only when it was out of sight did he turn around and knock on the door.

Brianna opened it with a grin. "Daddy is in the kitchen."

"It looks like you were helping," he said, looking at the flour covering the front of her.

"Mama was here, and she and I made cookies." Brianna scowled. "She wanted cut-out cookies and I wanted chocolate chip." Vin closed the door, and Brianna drew closer. "Mama's cookies are yucky." She curled her lip and then stuck out her tongue. "But I didn't tell her that because Daddy says I need to be nice." Vin held out his hand, and Brianna took it, half skipping as they made their way to the kitchen.

"Sorry I'm a little early. It didn't take as long as I thought to get here."

Casey patted the stool next to the counter, and Brianna climbed up. "Stir this dough, okay?" Casey flashed him a smile. "I'm glad you're here. Alicia just left."

"I saw her leaving… and I heard about the cookies." He gave Casey an approximation of Brianna's expression. "I bet she was happy."

"Mommy laughed, but she wasn't happy," Brianna said. Vin gave her credit—she was a smart little girl. "Daddy and I are making chocolate chip cookies." Apparently Alicia's favorites hadn't met with Casey's approval either. The scent of anise—a lot of it—still hung in the air. Casey handed him a single cookie, and Vin took a small bite and cringed at the overwhelming taste that burned his tongue a little. Then he tossed the cookie with the others.

"They taste like butt," Brianna said as she mixed the other dough.

He and Casey both tried not to laugh. "You shouldn't talk like that," Casey scolded lightly.

Brianna stopped mixing and looked up at Casey with those gorgeous eyes. "Well, they do." Her expression was so innocent that Vin had to turn away to get control of himself. He almost asked Brianna how she knew what butt tasted like. But this was definitely not the time for his dirty mind to run away with him.

"Okay, honey. Now let's get out the clean cookie sheets." Casey pulled the pans out, dropped the cookies onto them in perfect portions, then put them into the oven. "You can have some after dinner."

"Can I go play, then?" She climbed off the stool and took off toward the sunroom at the back of the house.

"She's something else," Vin said.

"That she is." Casey turned on him and drew Vin close and into a kiss that rivaled the heat in the oven. Vin let himself go with the tidal wave of passion until a soft crash of LEGOs followed by laughter broke through the cloud that had filled his mind. He pulled back slightly but stayed in Casey's strong arms.

"I know this is terrible timing, but how did the Alicia visit go?" Vin asked.

Casey shrugged. "She seems to think she can just drop in whenever she wants. I let her in this time because Brianna actually seemed engaged with her. They made awful cookies, as you know. Then, once that was done, she left. Alicia seemed happy…."

"Well, that only lasted until she reached the sidewalk. I get the feeling that Alicia is putting on some kind of act. By the time she reached the Mercedes, I could see that she was fuming. Maybe things aren't working out the way she wants, after all."

Casey sighed softly. "It doesn't matter. She can act however she wants. I send my lawyer a note after each visit with my thoughts about her behavior. I also let my lawyer know if Alicia calls first or just barges in. I have no idea what her game is, but I'm not playing it. I have full custody. And officially, Alicia doesn't even have visitation rights because she never showed up to any of the hearings. And she was well notified— the courts saw to that. I'm doing what's right because I want her and Brianna to have a relationship, but I won't give her free rein to do what she likes."

Vin nodded. "As long as you know."

"Was she driving?" Casey asked, and Vin shook his head.

"I didn't see who it was."

Tension filled Casey's arms. "I know who she's with. At least, I know his first name. But I'm trying to find out more. Carter is running the plates on his car. Once I find out his basic information, I can go from there. Two can play this game. Alicia got angry when she thought that I might be spending time with you, so I'm anxious to find out what kind of person she's spending her time with." He blew out a long breath and stepped back. "Let's talk about something more pleasant than my ex-wife, okay?"

Vin smiled. "Yes, please." He kissed Casey once more but pulled back when Brianna hurried in the room.

"Are the cookies done?" She jumped to try to look into the oven.

"In a minute." Casey lifted her so she could see through the oven door. "Go and play. I'll take them out soon, but then they need to cool. I'm going to start dinner, and you can have cookies afterward."

"What do you need me to do?" Vin asked.

"Keep me company," Casey answered as he turned off the oven. Then he pulled out the cookies and set them on a rack to cool. "Carter is working on the key we found. He thinks he might be able to find out the kind of vehicle and which year it was just with the key. Technology is great, isn't it? So we should be able to narrow down our search pretty quickly. It isn't like there's a BMW in every driveway in town."

Vin turned his chair so he could see Casey better. "True. It isn't something you see a lot of in town, especially late-model ones. Though it's possible these people don't actually live here. What if they're part of something bigger?"

Casey shrugged. "It's a distinct possibility. The pot-growing operation is pretty much small potatoes—though it's still illegal—but it's the prescription painkillers that are our main concern. Carlisle is a major transportation hub because of the highways. And with I-81 going the way it does, it allows product from the south to make it to New York and other big eastern cities without going through a bunch of cities the way I-95 does. It's sort of a back-door route. But still, I can't help feeling that the pot we found in the greenhouse was for local distribution and use." He began prepping green beans and potatoes for dinner.

Vin leaned forward. "I have to ask because… well, I have to. Why bother with the pot at all? Most people think it should be legal anyway. I know Pennsylvania has weird, old-fashioned laws, but is it really hurting anyone? Wouldn't your time be better spent elsewhere? I know you're going to think I'm stupid, but I'm just asking." He didn't want Casey to think he was being an asshole or something.

"I get asked that quite a bit, and I understand where you're coming from. But right now I'm enforcing the law. That's what I'm supposed to do. And it's not really about the pot—it's about the drugs. If someone was just growing weed, we'd probably look into it but not make it a high priority. But it's more than that. They turned your dad's greenhouse into a drug distribution center. They broke in and took it over. They've done that in other places as well, but up until now, all we found were the plants. A patch of marijuana was planted west of town in part of the state forest. We've found what was left of their operations in an older greenhouse west of town. Heck, they even planted the stuff in parts of one of the parks, off the hiking trails. These guys are bold, and their operation is expanding. We have to find them soon. I don't like the idea of Carlisle becoming known as the place to get your illegal drugs." It was clear that this was getting very frustrating for Casey.

"So what are we going to do about it?" Vin had been thinking about this a lot. "There has to be someone behind all this—one person has to be in charge. Likely someone with some experience growing the stuff. You don't just start doing this on a whim." He stood, peering over Casey's shoulder at the stove. "Where are they getting their seedling plants? And what's their source for the opioids?"

Casey paused in his chopping, putting his thoughts together. "For the plants, we think it could be a basement. It would take intense grow lights to get the crops to maturity, but a basement could be set up with constant rotation propagating the plants from seed. Three or four lights would do it, as long as it was warm enough. Start a batch, take them out to plant, then start another. Though enclosed places like your greenhouse are best around here—they provide a longer growing season. That's the angle we've been taking so far. But these dealers seem to be abandoning that line of business. There isn't as much money in it anymore, now that it's legal in so many places. Other channels are taking over. So they're moving on to harder substances."

"Damn," Vin said. "Casey… what if selling the pot isn't what these guys are doing?" He grew excited. "What if they were just plant wholesalers—with a network of buyers? And now they're using that same network to peddle the opiates you found?" It was a chilling thought and one that only added to the urgency.

Casey set down the knife and turned to stare at him. "What?"

"Think about it. Say you had a business that was drying up, so to speak. But you already had the distribution network in place. So why not abandon the product that's not in demand and shift to another that is?" He grinned as Casey thought over his idea. "What if growing pot was just the way they started out? They've made some money, and now they want more. So they shifted into selling prescription narcotics. It makes sense, don't you think?"

Brianna wandered in. "Daddy, I'm really hungry. My tummy hurts for a cookie."

Vin held out his arms, and Brianna came to him. He lifted her on his lap. "Daddy is making dinner right now, so you need to wait."

Casey turned around. "I'm going to put the meat on the grill." He tickled her, and Brianna squirmed and laughed. "You stay here and be good for Mr. Vin. No cookies before dinner, though, okay?" He grinned but held her gaze.

"I promise." She managed to sound like a put-upon teenager for a second. When Casey went out back, Brianna slipped down off his lap. "We could play with my dolls if you like."

"How about LEGOs?" Vin asked. "I'm better with those than I am with dolls."

"Because you're a boy?" she asked. "You know that boys can play with dolls." She put her hands on her hips as if daring him to argue with her.

"I know. But I played with LEGOs a lot when I was your age."

She thought a minute. "Okay. Can we make a cradle with LEGOs?"

Vin smiled. "I'll do my very best."

It turned out Brianna had a ton of LEGOs. Some of them appeared old enough to have been Casey's. Others were bright and new, but the bag they came in was huge. Brianna dumped them all on the floor, and Vin sat with her and tried to figure out how he was going to make a LEGO baby cradle. One thing he knew for sure—it was going to be big and colorful.

"I like the pink ones best," Brianna said, immediately setting her doll aside and searching through the stack of bricks. Someone had gotten her a lot of different colors, and it didn't take long for the stack of pink ones to pile up. "Then the purple and white." She stacked those as well, each color in its own pile. "Use those, please." If he had to predict, he'd say that Brianna was going to grow up to be a general.

Casey came in and leaned against the doorframe, his arms crossed over his chest. "You need to be nice to Mr. Vin. We want him to like us. Being bossy is not the way to make friends."

"I wasn't, Daddy. I was just showing him what to do. My teacher says that we should all try to be leaders now and then." She turned back to Vin. "See? I'm leading you to the right color LEGOs." She patted his shoulder and then went back to her dolls. Vin turned to Casey, who shook his head, looking upward as though he expected some sort of divine help.

"Okay. Let me see if I can figure this out." Vin started working out how he was going to make what he had promised.

"You know you don't have to do this," Casey said from behind him.

But Vin was enjoying it, and once he figured out how he was going to make the cradle, the design came together pretty easily. "It's going to be fun." His belly fluttered as Casey rested his hands on his shoulder. Vin patted one of them and looked back to share a smile with Casey before returning to his task. By the time dinner was ready, it was almost done.

"Come to dinner," Casey told him when he didn't get up right away. Vin got to his feet, leaving his creation on the floor, then joined Brianna at the table. Brianna snagged a green bean and popped it into her mouth, receiving a scowl from Casey.

Once everything was set, they passed around the food, with Casey helping Brianna. She seemed to want to take a lot, but Casey only allowed her small portions. "You can have more if you eat it all," he told her, and she got to work. The kid had a good appetite and tucked right in.

Casey's phone vibrated on the table, and he snatched it up. "Grandma doesn't allow phones while we're eating," Brianna said.

"Your daddy has to keep his phone with him because of work," Vin told her gently as Casey answered the message.

Apparently, though, it wasn't a single-text issue. Casey kept messaging, his expression darkening by the second. Clearly he wasn't happy with whatever

was being said. Finally he set the phone aside, and
when another message came in, he slipped the phone
into his pocket without answering.

"How is the beef?" Casey asked. He'd made a
flank steak and had cut the pieces really thin.

"Perfect," Vin told him. "The marinade is amazing." They shared a smile as Brianna continued eating
without stop. She seemed to think the same thing.

"Brianna was always an eater," Casey said and
turned to her. "When you were hungry, you let us
know."

"When I was a baby?" she asked before taking
another bite.

"Yup. You were a pretty baby, but you were always hungry. We'd give you a bottle, and you'd suck
it down hard before falling to sleep." Casey pushed
a few strands of hair out of Brianna's face. "You
were a wonderful baby, just like you're an amazing
daughter." He stroked her head and then returned to
his dinner.

The potatoes were good, and the beans amazing
with a touch of onion and maybe some garlic. There
was plenty, and Casey kept passing food Vin's way.
By the time dinner was over, the dishes were nearly
empty and Vin was stuffed full. Brianna, on the other
hand, kept eyeing the cookies, and Casey gave her
one before sending her off to play. Vin stayed behind
to help clear the table. Casey put the few leftovers in
the refrigerator, then loaded the dishwasher.

"Alicia was messaging," Casey said. "She wanted to see Brianna tomorrow afternoon. Brianna will
be at my parents', and they are not going to let Alicia

anywhere near her or them. They hate her for leaving, and she isn't welcome in their house. I told her she could come over on Wednesday for a few hours." Casey sighed. "That's when I put the phone away."

"I'm guessing that the messages kept coming," Vin said.

Casey nodded. "Yeah." He pulled out his phone, scanned the messages, and sent one final one. "Tonight I'll download these and send them over to my lawyer. She can file them with the rest of Alicia's PITA rants. I'm really starting to think that we were all better off when she was staying away. I want Brianna to have a relationship with her, but Bri's life can't revolve around Alicia's whims. It's like she's trying to make up for two years of ignoring her in a single week."

"Maybe that's exactly what she's doing. Did she say how long she was going to stay?" Vin asked.

"Another week, maybe. She said Renaldo has business here in town with a Nathan Something-or-Other that he needs to attend to. She sounded pissed when she said his name, as if the guy was taking Renaldo's attention away from her." Casey was clearly curious about this Renaldo and what he might be up to. "Anyway, her rant seems to have ended for now." He closed the dishwasher door and started it. "I'm starting to think Alicia is losing touch with the real situation, but as long as she's acting this way, I'm not going to let her see Brianna. I always thought that a little girl should know her mother, but maybe I was wrong. Brianna deserves better."

"No good deed goes unpunished," Vin said softly, and Casey nodded his agreement. "Let's go in with Brianna and do something fun." He held out his hand, and Casey took it.

"Good idea."

"HAVE YOU ever thought of getting a pet for her?" Vin asked as they sat in the backyard, under the shade of an old maple tree.

"Yes. But I think she's too young yet, and with the hours I work, I'd hate to leave a dog alone for that long. My mother is not a fan of animals or I'd have gotten her a pup she could take along when she went to my mother's."

"Is that why you never had a pet?"

Casey nodded. "But you had that little terrier mix that your mom brought home."

"Ulysses. Yes. Mom found him at the shop, huddled outside. She brought him in, and that was all there was to it. She tried to find his owner, but we got a dog instead." His mother had always had a huge heart, especially when it came to animals. "He was so much fun. Remember taking him for walks?"

Casey chuckled. "Yeah, and we usually brought him home wet and caked with mud. That dog loved romping down by the creek. He was a really good dog." He stared out across the yard. "You know, I'd really love a dog, and I know Brianna would too. Alicia had allergies, so she and I never got one."

Brianna came over from where she'd been playing with some of her dolls on the grass and climbed onto Casey's lap. He held her, and she leaned against him. "Are you getting tired?" Casey asked. "How about you have a cookie and then after a while, we get you ready for bed." She was flagging. Vin and Casey talked quietly as Brianna's energy ebbed.

Vin excused himself and used the bathroom. He returned with a few cookies that he gave to Brianna. She ate one and then yawned widely and gave the other one to Casey.

"Wait here. I'll be back once I get her to bed." Casey left, and Vin sat there, enjoying the summer evening air. A slight breeze rustled the leaves over his head. Vin closed his eyes as thoughts of Casey and what the two of them were about to do filled his mind. They had both confessed to teenage interest, and God, Vin hoped he didn't turn out to be a disappointment. It was so easy to get things all worked up in his head. And if he fell short…. He groaned, pushing away the pressure he was putting on himself.

After all these years and God knows how many late-night fantasies, he was going to get a chance to step out of his dreams and into reality. That had to be worlds better than anything his own mind could conjure up.

"She went to sleep almost as soon as her head hit the pillow. Between Alicia and everything else that's happened today, I think she's just worn out." Casey sank into his chair. "Do you want something to drink? I don't know about you, but I could use a beer."

"Sure." Vin followed Casey with his gaze, loving the way he walked. What a perfect evening. A flock of birds settled in the tree above him, chirping between themselves. When Casey returned, he handed Vin an opened bottle and tipped his to his lips.

"Sometimes I wonder how much I can take. Alicia leaving was bad enough, but now that she's back, I'd kind of like her to leave again." He took another swig of his beer. "I know I shouldn't let her get to me, but that's easier said than done."

"You used to love her. Those feelings still have to be in there, in some way," Vin offered, trying to understand himself.

"I did care for her, yes. And when we got married, things were happy for a time. We had Brianna right away, and Alicia was a good mother. She sure loved Brianna. But…." Casey drained the last of his beer and set the bottle aside. "I don't know what happened. I thought it was postpartum depression, but I don't know. She became moody six months or so after Brianna was born, and it lasted a long time. Then, all of a sudden, she seemed to be more like herself again. Brianna was learning to walk and then saying her first words. We were a happy family."

"Except…," Vin prompted.

"I don't know. I think it was me. I was starting to figure some things out, and there were things that didn't fit. But I ignored them. I had a lovely wife and a daughter I adored. I didn't want to hurt either of them, so I kept my worries and insecurities to myself. I mean, we had a nice life, and I like to think we were happy. But something was missing. I didn't blame Alicia, and I still don't. But we were together for a lot of years…."

Vin leaned forward in the chair, slowly sipping his beer, then offering the rest to Casey. He seemed to need it. "What really happened?"

Casey sighed. "I don't know. We were happy. Yes, I was… unsettled, but I thought I hid it well. Then all of sudden, Alicia told me that she was leaving to go back home and that it was my fault. I don't know. Maybe…."

Vin took his hand. "Sometimes people just know what they have to do. Maybe Alicia wasn't happy. If she had been, she wouldn't have left." He was beginning to think that Alicia leaving had less to do with Casey and more to do with Alicia and what she wanted. In his opinion, this was more of a power play on her part than anything to do with Casey and Brianna. Maybe she had just decided to make Casey as miserable as possible, and this was how she was trying to do it.

"I think that maybe you've carried a lot of guilt that wasn't yours. Alicia made her own decision. Yes, she may try to blame you, but no one forced her to leave. And nobody made her stay away for all this time." He squeezed Casey's fingers. "I think that you need to let go of whatever regret you're holding. Alicia's decisions are hers—not yours." Vin hoped that Casey could just let them go, but he knew things like this didn't just go *poof* and disappear. Guilt was powerful, and sometimes it refused to let go.

"I suppose you could be right. But shouldn't I have been able to make my wife happy?" Casey asked.

Vin shrugged. "If you weren't happy in the marriage—if you were looking inward to find what you really wanted—how could you have made her happy?" Vin took Casey's hand. "What I'm saying is that maybe Alicia was searching for something the same way you were." It seemed pretty obvious to him. Vin doubted that a contented person simply left their husband and child without warning. "You're a good man; you always were. As kids, we got into mischief, but it was you who always pulled us back when we were on the verge of going too far. You take care of your daughter and love her to death. And seeing you in your uniform…." He swallowed hard as that image flashed in his head. "I always had a thing for a man in uniform."

Casey leaned forward in his chair. "You did?" He tilted his head forward in such a way that his eyes caught the light from the back of the house, and they sparkled for just a second. Then the effect passed, but not the warmth that instantly made the air sultry and close.

"Oh yeah." Vin shook his head and tried to change the subject. "I'm still trying to figure out how we lost touch."

Casey stood. "That's pretty easy. You went your way, and I went mine. I was busy caring for a wife and Brianna, trying to make a living. You were making your way out in California, and distance and time took their toll." Casey took small steps closer. "But we aren't far apart right now." His swallowed and licked his lips. Damn, Vin wanted to suck on that tongue and abuse Casey's pretty lips until they were swollen and everyone knew he'd been kissed to within an inch of his life. Hell, that thought sent yet another wave of fire rushing through Vin, and he didn't want to step away. This heat was magnetic, pulling him closer to the flame.

"No, we aren't. I'm right here." He wasn't sure how long he'd be able to stay, but dammit, Vin intended to make the very most of the time they had. Vin drew Casey into his arms, closing their lips together. Fuck, Casey was strong, and once he added his embrace, Vin knew he was sunk. The way Casey held him, kissed him, was just like he'd always imagined: firm, strong, with barely controlled power. Vin pressed harder, and Casey held firm, meeting his kisses, increasing the intensity until Vin's head spun. Before he really realized it, they were moving along the walk toward the back door. "I want you all to myself, and I don't intend to share you. Not even with the birds."

Casey pulled open the door and let them inside. They moved quietly through the house, with Casey locking up and turning out lights as they went. Then Casey took Vin's hand and led him up the stairs, past a grandfather clock on the landing that ticked softly in the quiet house. Once they reached the top, Casey opened the door to his bedroom and ushered Vin inside. "I'll be right back. I promise."

Vin went inside as Casey continued down the narrow hall, most likely to check on Brianna. Once in the bedroom, Vin looked around. The room was neat, exceedingly so, with a dresser, bed, and nightstand. The soft gray walls were the perfect canvas for the framed drawings that Brianna had given him. Vin looked them over—the progression from scribbles to finger paint to actual drawings was incredibly beautiful. "The domain of a proud father," Vin said when Casey came inside and closed the door.

"Brianna is asleep, so maybe for the next few hours, I can be something other than a father." Casey turned out the overhead light, plunging the room into darkness. Then there was a snick, and a soft light from the top of the dresser bathed the room in the ambiance for romance. Vin turned as Casey pulled up the hem of his shirt, stretching his muscular arms over his head, elongating his torso. He was gorgeous, his warm skin dancing as it moved in the light. Vin didn't wait for him to finish but moved closer, the urge to touch becoming overwhelming.

Casey was all smooth skin, rippled with muscles that flowed and stretched with each movement. Vin continued his exploration, kissing Casey, touching every inch of skin Casey revealed. And when Casey turned to him, opening the buttons on Vin's shirt and parting the fabric, Vin stood there and let him. Casey's heated hands brushed over Vin's belly and upward, his knuckles bumping one of his nipples. Without pulling away, Vin hissed, and Casey did it again.

Vin's head was spinning, and Casey held his gaze, stilling for just a few seconds. Vin held his breath, waiting for what Casey would do next. Every cell in his being was on edge, his heart pausing a split second in anticipation. Casey smoothed Vin's shirt off his shoulders and then pushed it down his arms and tossed it aside. Then he wound his arms around him. Casey's intense scent filled Vin's nose and made his head spin even more. Then, with a slight bump of his chest, Casey pulled him close, skin to skin. "This is what I've wanted for a long time," Casey whispered, cutting off any argument with a hard kiss.

Vin's head started to swim, and all of a sudden he didn't know which way was up. But it didn't matter—Casey had him. He must have been falling, but the mattress met him, and Casey came right along with him. His weight was stunningly wonderful as Vin sank deeper into passion he never wanted to end.

"Casey…," Vin murmured, knowing he had to be quiet, yet screaming inside his own head because he wanted more.

Casey seemed to understand, because he took Vin's hands and tugged them up over his head. "Quiet is the name of the game," he whispered an inch from Vin's ear. A ripple of desire raced through Vin in response.

"I have to warn you that I am rarely quiet in bed," Vin told him, finding it hard to contain his excitement.

Casey's eyes glistened. "I always imagined you as a screamer. So here's the deal. As long as you're quiet, we can continue. But if you make a lot of noise, we'll have to stop. Because the last thing either of us wants is for Brianna to come in here. I wish I had one of those daughters who could sleep through a hurricane, but that's not my little girl. Okay?" Vin nodded his response. "Excellent. Now that I have you in my bed, I have to figure out what to do with you."

"What do you want to do?" Vin whispered.

Casey wet his lips, and Vin followed the motion with his eyes, mesmerized. "It's…. I don't know. This was something I used to fantasize about when I was in bed, at night, when the house was quiet and no one was around. It's almost like I can't believe it's real."

"Well, it is," Vin whispered in return, pulling down his arms when Casey released them. "So what do you want? I'm right here, and I'm not going anywhere. You and I have all night."

Casey held his gaze. "I know. But what happens after tonight? What about at the end of the week when you go home? Brianna already likes you, and…." He closed his eyes, and Vin smoothed his hands over Casey's head.

"I don't know. Sometimes we just have to take what we're given." His father was right. This was a second chance for them, and Vin wanted to make the most of it, even if he wished it could be something more lasting. Maybe Casey and Brianna could come see in him LA on school breaks, and he could spend his vacations in Carlisle. It might be possible to do the long-distance thing if they both wanted it badly enough. Lord knows Vin did. There had to be a way to make it work. He just needed some time to consider the possibilities. "We need to make the most of the time we have." He drew Casey downward, capturing his lips. Casey tasted amazing, with just a hint of beer. "We can stop if that's what you want to do." God, he hoped the answer was no.

Casey shook his head and slipped off the bed. "Get up there." His eyes were wide and his breathing heavy. Casey unhooked his belt and pulled it off, popping open his pants. Vin didn't need to be told twice, shucking his shoes and jeans in a matter of seconds. He was about to slip out of the last of his clothing when Casey pounced, pinning him to the bed. Vin gasped and then snapped his mouth shut. If quiet was what Casey needed, then that was what he was going to get. But that didn't mean Vin was going to be passive.

Vin groaned and shivered as Casey felt his way along his body. The man seemed on a mission to find Vin's special spots, and so far he was on his way to discovering all of them. The base of Vin's neck was always sensitive, though the area just above his hipbone was a place most guys didn't know about. But Casey sure as hell did. He teased Vin, kissing here, nipping there, while all Vin could do was squirm on the bedding, his breathing coming in pants, cock desperate to be released from its cotton confines. Casey might have the patience of a saint, but at the moment, Vin's was running out.

"Remember to be quiet," Casey cautioned him. Obviously he could see how close to the edge Vin was.

"How can I do that when you're driving me crazy over here?" They weren't even naked yet and Vin was already at the end of his rope. If Casey continued this way all night, Vin would be nothing more than a puddle of goo come morning.

Casey learned close, his warm breath tickling Vin's ear. "Then tell me what you want. You're the experienced one here, remember?"

"You want me to spell it out?" Vin asked. The guys he'd been with in California were usually so anxious to get on with it that they barely took the time to get their clothes off before someone was sucking or fucking something. Vin almost didn't know what to do with Casey's patience. It was refreshing and frustrating at the same time.

"Oh, sweetheart, I intend to suck your brains out through your dick. If that's all you want, we can get right down to it," Casey said and met his gaze, and he shivered. "But there's plenty of time for that." Casey wrapped him in his arms, rolling Vin on the bed so he was now on top. Not that it mattered. Because it seemed Casey could top from the bottom. He slipped his huge hands down Vin's back, continuing lower, passing over his buttcheeks, then slipping his fingers under the elastic of his briefs… and going lower still. Vin could hardly breathe, he was so excited.

"Jesus. You seem to get off on doing everything really slowly. Don't you know you're killing me?" Vin asked as Casey continued pushing Vin's underwear down until Vin was able to wiggle out of them. Naked, he got to work on Casey's clothes, and within seconds, they were skin to skin.

"There's no need to hurry. You're worth taking the time. And I want to feel and taste every part of you."

But Vin had had enough. In anything else, Casey could go as slow as he wanted. But when Casey was with him, this habit needed to die. Sure, he liked that Casey wanted to take the time to make their intimate night together special. But there was only so much a man could take.

Vin rolled off Casey and lay on the bedding. "Then here I am."

Casey leaned over him, his eyes sparkling in the low light. "I can see that. And I see you."

Vin understood where that came from. "Not many people did back then."

"I always did." Casey leaned closer, his tongue circling a nipple. Vin panted. "I just wish I'd had the guts to do something about it."

Vin wound his fingers in Casey's short hair, arching his back to get a little more pressure. He hissed as Casey lightly used his teeth, then soothed the area with his tongue before moving on. Vin lost all track of time, not that it mattered. Casey was a master at figuring out what Vin liked and then capitalizing on driving him out of his mind. This was more than he had ever dreamed sex could be. And when Casey reached his cock, Vin only hoped he didn't disgrace himself and go off like a teenager. It took all the control he had to hold back as Casey lowered his lips around Vin's cock, taking him deeper, adding sensation after sensation until Vin could hardly breathe.

His control slipped away by inches. Casey whittled away at it little by little, until his body didn't even feel like his own. And still Casey persisted, until Vin could take no more. He groaned more loudly than he'd intended, and Casey stilled. "What's wrong?" The clouds that had been filling his mind slowly parted, and he blinked at Casey. "Was I too loud?"

"No," Casey breathed and kissed him, pressing their bodies together once again. Heat surrounded him, and Vin held on as Casey thrust his hips. Vin met each movement, and as the last of his remaining control snapped, he tumbled into his release, clinging to Casey to keep from flying to pieces as Casey came right behind him.

It took Vin a while to come back to himself, but when he did, he realized that Casey was holding him in his strong arms. Casey's embrace made him feel safe, something he'd never felt before with other guys—something he'd never realized he'd even wanted. But it was pretty amazing to be able to just let go. So he just kept his eyes closed and let himself savor the moment.

This sense of calm was almost foreign to him. In LA, things moved fast. His customers always had to be right, and they wanted everything yesterday. Almost everyone he encountered in his field thought they were important and that he should be thrilled to give them what they wanted. Not having that pressure right now felt so good.

Casey rolled on the mattress with Vin still in his arms. Vin rested his head on Casey's shoulder, and with a soft sigh, he closed his eyes and quickly dropped off to sleep.

CHAPTER 6

"LES, WHAT are you doing here?" Casey asked as he climbed the steps to the station the following morning. Vin had left the house before Brianna had gotten up, so to her—if not to Casey—it was just another morning. After breakfast, he'd taken his daughter to his mother's house for the day.

Les slowly climbed the steps using his cane. He had been injured on the job a few years earlier. That accident had cost him his career as an officer, though he still worked with the police, usually as a consultant. "I heard you had an interesting case brewing with your drug distributors," he answered. "I called the chief, and he invited me in to see if I could help you guys figure this out."

Casey was thrilled for any help he could get. "Another perspective will be very welcome. I've been doing a lot of thinking about this case, and I might have come up with a new angle. Can I run it by you?" He held open the door so Les could go inside. Then he checked himself in and led Les back to one of the conference rooms, where Les lowered himself into a chair.

"Okay. What do you have?" Les asked.

Casey laid out the facts as they knew them, with Les nodding as he took it in.

"What do you think is happening?"

"Well, we've been operating under the supposition that the growers turned opioid distributors are a group of people hedging their bets and spreading the risk," Casey explained, and Les rolled his eyes. Clearly he didn't think much of the idea.

"But I've been thinking," Casey added. "We seem to have a shifting business model here. There's a lot of money in selling opioids and other drugs. Pot growers are usually small-time felons. Because it's legal in so much of the country, nobody really worries about it, and the growers can usually get away with it pretty easily. But this shift in operations shows a level of sophistication and business savvy that you don't find in your average pot grower. Whoever is behind this isn't stupid, and they have to have factored in the possibility of some losses. That's pretty sharp-thinking stuff. And it tells us we're up against someone who can think on their feet, and likely has a large amount of money at their disposal."

Les nodded. "I can see that. What other ideas do you have?"

Red and Carter joined them, taking seats at the table. Casey did a quick update on their conversation before continuing. "We think there's a network involved. And we might have discovered one of their major distribution centers."

Les leaned forward. "A distribution operation has real possibilities, but it's going to be more difficult to nail down. What we really need is more information." He seemed to ponder the situation. "What does your friend know about all this?"

Casey's hackles rose. "He's been cleared, if that's what you're getting at. Vin just got into town a few days ago. His father hadn't been out to the greenhouse in months, and he's the one who called us. I doubt it was either of them." Red gave him a smile, and Casey calmed himself. They needed to work together. Casey needed to remember that they were all part of the same team.

"Which greenhouse?" Les asked levelly.

"The one from Robins Flowers, behind East Ridge."

Red smiled. "I used to go there as a kid. It was really nice. My aunt used to shop there all the time before it closed." He sighed.

Carter nodded. "That's where I bought flowers for Don once. They were good people, and the older lady in there was something else. She'd talk your ear off sometimes, and you always left with more flowers than you intended to buy. I swear she could sell saltwater to a sailor."

"The dealers broke in, then set up their plants on the floor of the greenhouse. But more importantly, it looks like they used the place as a distribution point for opiates. Right now we're working on finding out who might have known it was empty. The fact that the business was closed is common knowledge, and it looked neglected, so I suspect the perps figured it was safe to use." Casey paused, then looked at Carter. "Did you have any luck with the key fob we found?"

"Not so far. I've nailed down the years from 2006 to 2011 based on the design and basic compatibility. I'm running a search to see what I can come up with, but I suspect the list is going to be large enough that it may not tell us anything. Also, the key fob itself is hosed. I'm trying to fix it so if we find a candidate, we can confirm it's the car we're after."

Les sat quietly. "Do you have a list of locations where you've found plants in the past? Before these guys shifted their business?" Casey nodded. "Then I'd start back at the oldest ones to make sure they aren't being used again for new activities. Sometimes people are just that bold. From there, let's try to think like these guys. Where would you put a drug distribution operation?"

"A location that's out of the way, yet close to a good road and the freeway if possible," Casey offered.

"And a location where cars coming and going isn't going to be noticed too easily," Les added, and Casey turned to Red and Carter.

"We need to check out the old watercress farm up the Letort Spring Run. There's access to a good road, and I'm sure some of the old buildings aren't being used. People walk out there a lot on the rail trail. Also, behind Thornwald Park, there are wooded areas with trails that people use all the time. I remember there was a fire back there that cleared an area before the flames could be put out. And there's easy access to the freeway at the back of the trail."

Les nodded. "And we should try up by the Expo Center as well. That area seems to fit the bill too. If we're lucky, we'll catch a break." He sighed and rubbed his leg. "I wish I was up to checking out these locations with you, but Dex would kill me. And I'm scheduled to read to the kids at Hummingbird Books later. You should bring Brianna in again. She loved it last time."

"I'll do that," Casey said. Les levered himself up and left the conference room, heading toward the chief's office. "We may as well get on it."

"I need to check on my computer searches and make sure they're running. Why don't you two go ahead? I'll let you know if I come up with something." Carter left the room, and Red led Casey out to the car.

"I'll drive," Red said, and they headed out.

The areas near the Expo Center looked the same. It turned out there wasn't the space to hide anything, and it was very open, so they ruled that out quickly. The clearing at the back of Thornwald near the highway looked the same as it always did, with the remnants of the burned trees decaying on the ground. It hadn't been disturbed, and other than some trash that Casey stuffed in the plastic bag he carried with him for just such an occasion, there was no evidence of any disturbances or unusual activity in the woods. From there, they checked the other locations they'd found near town before… but there were no signs that they were being used as drop zones for narcotics. One area had been taken over as a community vegetable garden, which tickled Casey to no end. The pot farmers had cleared a small area, and in the end, the local people benefited. Things didn't usually work out so well.

"Let's head out to the watercress farm. I'll alert the state police that we're heading that way and that we'll contact them if we find anything," Casey said, then made the call in to their dispatchers. Pennsylvania was a patchwork of jurisdictions, and the various departments had to work together on many occasions.

"I've walked the trail along the creek many times, but Terry and I rarely come this far," Red said as he turned off the main road. They drove on back to where the road crossed the stream. Red slowed, but instead of stopping, he continued on, turned left, then headed back toward town. "I think that maybe this evening, we should take a walk along the trail instead." They shared a look, and Casey nodded. "I noticed people on top of one of the hills to the south, and there were a couple of flashes between the trees," Red added.

"Good idea." They were outside their jurisdiction anyway. If they found something or came across suspects, they wouldn't be able to arrest them. They'd have to wait for the state police. So it made more sense to poke around on their own and do their best not to raise suspicions. Hopefully they would actually get somewhere. "You know, there's a hill closer to town that might give us a better view of that area. And from there we wouldn't be seen. And it's inside the borough, so we wouldn't have to worry about stepping on any toes."

"Let's talk to the chief and see what he says," Red agreed.

Forgoing their walk, they drove back to the station. Inside, they found Carter at his computer. "I came across a few leads on the car, but not many, I'm afraid. There are a few of those years' models in town that we can check out. And I got the fob working, so if we locate the cars, we'll be able to see if the fob is a match. I printed out the registered addresses. Did you find anything?"

"Maybe. We need to talk to the chief. But it's possible one of the hills above the old farm out there has some activity. We thought we'd take a walk out there to check it out. Maybe get a buddy in the state police to join us. See if there is something interesting out there without scaring anyone away."

"Go ask him, and if he agrees, then I'm game to go too," Carter said.

"Terry and I could use a walk. And you could bring Vin." Red grinned, and Casey wondered if that was his clumsy way of matchmaking. "Go see what the chief says."

"LET ME get this straight," Vin said when Casey called him later. "You want to get together later and go for a walk in the woods so you and the guys can check out something suspicious?" He sounded skeptical. "You really know how to sweep a guy off his feet, don't you? A walk under the trees, you and I

together with some friends, just the sound of birds…
and guns, just in case."

"Oh, well, I'm sorry… I…," Casey stammered.

"What time are you picking me up, you great big
romantic? If nothing else, it will be a date I'm not
likely to ever forget."

"We'll go to dinner afterwards. Brianna and
Mom have a dance thing they do on Mondays. It
could be nice."

Vin snickered. "As long as there's no gunplay.
Though you know I'm up for playing with the right
weapon. Lots of fireworks." His voice was almost
gravelly, and Casey stifled a groan. He was at his
desk and didn't want the guys to guess at the sugges-
tive things Vin was saying.

"Six?" he asked.

"I'll be loaded and ready when you are," Vin
told him. "Is this one of those times when we have to
be circumspect, or…?"

"The people coming with us are all friends." He
had to keep his voice down. "I'll see you then." Casey ended the call as Red approached his desk. "All
set. We'll meet where the trail starts near the school
at six."

"Perfect. It's supposed to be a nice evening,"
Red told him with a wink.

Casey really liked the men he worked with, but
some of them could be a little too pushy. Red figured
that since he was blissfully happy, everyone else
should be. And the huge man was not above giving
a little push when necessary. It wasn't as if Casey
didn't want to have someone in his life. He had been

alone for a long time now. But honestly, he was sure Vin wasn't going to stay, and things were going to be hard enough when Vin left to go back to LA.

"Good." He turned to the paperwork on his desk, determined to get it done before he left for the night.

VIN WAS all smiles when he answered the door. "I'm ready for our little expedition if you are." He grinned, and Casey wondered what Vin had up his sleeve. Before closing the door, he grabbed a cloth grocery bag and told his father he was going. Then he descended the stairs and headed down the walk. "Aren't you coming?"

"What's all this?" Casey asked.

"We're going on a hike, and that means provisions. I've got water and soda, trail mix, some granola bars, and grapes."

Casey snickered. "You know we're only going a little over a mile each way. We're not trekking the Himalayas."

Vin stopped. "Do you want me to take this back?"

"Nope." Casey took the bag. "Come on. If we're going to go for an arduous hike, we'll need provisions." Yeah, he was having a little fun with Vin, but it was kind of him to bring snacks. Knowing Red and the guys, the food would be gone long before they reached the end of the trail.

They walked to the corner, where the guys were already waiting at the start of the trail. "Vin, you know Red, right? This is his partner, Terry, and

Carter's better half, Donald." They all shook hands. "Where are the kids?"

"Alex is playing with the neighbor boy. He insists he's too old for a babysitter," Donald said. "That's okay. I pay their oldest to keep an eye on him. I'm happy, and Alex is happy and none the wiser." They started down the path. "So, what's the plan?"

"When we get close to the area, we'll take a trek through the woods to the overlook. If there is something, we'll call it in. If not, we'll keep going," Casey explained. "Either way, we get to scarf down the snacks Vin brought. It's like he knew we can eat at any time."

Vin rolled his eyes. "You're guys. Of course you can eat." Then he strode ahead, and Casey hurried to catch up. Vin took his arm, and they started down the trail at the edge of the school property before the shadows of the woods engulfed them.

The trail was lined with trees and shrubs, some in bloom with the most amazing scent. It seemed to fill the air and hang on the breeze. Red and Terry hurried past them, laughing as they chased one another, a couple in love, playing. Casey found himself smiling as they walked.

"Which of those two is actually faster?" Vin asked.

"In the water, it's definitely Terry. And he has the gold medals to prove it. In this situation? Probably Terry as well, though I don't think he really wants to get away."

Vin sighed. "I don't think I do either." He turned, and his warm gaze met Casey's.

"Come on, you lovebirds. You're falling behind," Red teased, so Casey picked up the pace. Red was right. They had some distance to cover and they needed to get out there. Still, it was nice just taking a walk.

"Did you do this sort of thing with Alicia?" Vin asked.

"Good God, no. Alicia liked her exercise and plants indoors." Casey chuckled. "I once took her camping, and she stayed in the screen house the whole time. She said there were too many bugs." He leaned close. "I really wonder how she manages in Costa Rica. Now that's a country with *bugs*. Thank God that isn't my problem anymore." Casey shrugged, and they continued walking.

The path led under the freeway and then continued south along the Letort Spring Run, eventually passing by a quarry and then a bridge over the stream. "We need to veer off here," Carter explained when they reached a path that intersected with theirs. "Casey, Red, and I are going to head up there and see if we can get the view we need. You three continue on as far as you like and then return. We'll figure things out from there."

They agreed, and Carter led the way along the partially overgrown path. After about two hundred yards, they began to climb. Just as Casey hoped, the top of the rise had been cleared some time ago, and they had a view of the spring run valley.

"Right over there," Casey said, pointing, and Red pulled out a small pair of binoculars to sight the area.

"There is definitely something going on. The area has been cleared. Maybe a plot fifty feet square at most. It gets good light, I'd guess, but it's fairly protected, and there's nothing around." He lowered the binoculars and handed them to Casey, who peered through.

"It's hard to tell if they've planted or not. It looks like it, but I can't tell what they are. The plants are too small. And the clearing is empty right now. I don't see anyone around." Casey passed the binoculars to Carter. "I think we need to continue on out there. I'd like to see if we can find their water source. They'll need some sort of pump, and if we can find it, then we'll have a further indication of what they're doing."

"I agree," Red said. "Let's get down and meet the guys. We can continue our walk, see if we can find their water source, and then report what we have to the state police. They'll have to take charge because we've passed out of our jurisdiction."

They retraced their steps and met their partners on the trail. After a quick confab, the group continued on, rounding the curve into the open area that had once been a watercress farm. The remains of the growing pens and water management systems could still be seen, but it was pretty much derelict. The stream was to the left, so they paid attention as they went, looking for some sort of pump or line rising from the opposite bank.

"Anything?" Vin asked quietly.

"There," Terry said without pointing. "Just up ahead. It looks like there's a hole of some sort, and a brown hose comes out of the water. It's partially buried." And there it was. The hose would have been invisible if it hadn't had a yellow stripe in the rubber.

Once he looked, he could see the pump under the water. "How do they power it?"

"I bet there's a solar panel on the south side of the clearing, just at the top of the hill. It's probably mounted to a tree. They maybe can get enough power from that and a battery to run the pump long enough to water the plants," Vin said. "It's just a guess, but I did something like that in LA to help a client with their garden, only we used cisterns and other second-ary-source water to irrigate the plants."

Casey stopped and gave himself a chance to think. "This doesn't look like any sort of distribution operation. Do you think it's the last piece of the oper-ation before they shifted to a new product?"

Red shrugged. "If it was me, I'd have ceased all old operations and concentrated on the new business. A smaller footprint means less chance of detection. So this could be completely unrelated, and we uncovered it because we were looking for something else. Who knows? We'll get it investigated and see if it leads us anywhere. But I have a feeling it's a dead end."

"We need to head back," Casey cautioned. The group all turned and walked back toward town. "Don't even look up toward the area. If someone is watching, we don't want to draw any attention to it. Let's just walk home."

"Thanks for coming," he said to Vin. "I know this probably wasn't your idea of a walk through the park."

"Are you kidding?" Vin asked with a grin. "I got to be part of a police investigation. Heck, I usually spend my days taking orders and arranging flowers.

Sure, I'm really good at it, and I make some stunning creations, but this was exciting." He grinned as they rounded the curve away from the area in question.

Red called in what they found to the other jurisdictions. As they continued down the trail, he let the others know that the state police would share what they found, but apparently they were already aware of the plot. They'd been watching the area, hoping to get enough evidence before moving forward.

"Wyatt, my contact in the state police, said there's been no sign of outside organization. They believe it's a just couple of local boys doing some growing." Casey was disappointed, but he supposed it was to be expected. His cases were never that easy.

"What do we do next?"

"Dinner?" Terry asked. "We could go to Molly Pitcher." Terry popped some grapes in his mouth. It seemed the guys had been munching on Vin's snacks while the cops had been climbing. "The beer is good, and so is the food."

"Then let's go," Vin said, peering into the bag he'd brought. "It seems someone has quite an appetite." Terry blushed. "What I want to know is, where do you put it?"

Red wrapped an arm around Terry's shoulders. "He has hollow arms and legs. But he's so cute, I don't care."

They all continued down the trail, passing under the highway once again. Once they reached the trailhead, Casey said, "We'll meet you at the restaurant in fifteen minutes. I need to make a call and stop at the house." He needed to change his footwear and check that Brianna was okay. "Do you want to ride with me?" he asked Vin, who nodded, then walked over to the car and slid into the passenger seat.

A few minutes later, Casey pulled up in front of the house.

"I've been waiting for you. I'd like to see Brianna and I'll go through you if I have to," Alicia said, charging up the sidewalk at him.

"As you can see, she isn't here. Brianna is with my mother at their weekly dance class. If you had called, you'd have known that." His patience was running low. "And as I already told you, I'm working, and Brianna has a schedule of her own that I'm not going to change for you. We arranged for you to see her on Wednesday." He looked up and down the street. "Why are you here now? And where is Renaldo?" The man always seemed to be lurking somewhere close by, like a dark shadow following Alicia.

She ignored the question. "I'd really like to see Brianna." Her tone was so sweet, sugar wouldn't melt in her mouth.

Vin got out of the car, and Alicia's attention turned to him with an Arctic expression. "Can we help you?"

"I'm not sure what you hope to gain by acting this way. Custody of Brianna was decided long ago, in our divorce settlement. Remember? It was the one you neglected to show up for. And now you think you can just be with her whenever you want? Why is that? What is it you think you can get?"

She drew closer. "I found a really good lawyer, and he says I have a very good chance of being granted visitation, at least. After all, when I left, I was so stressed that I was making myself ill. I wasn't able to properly care for Brianna. But I got treatment in Costa Rica, and I can care for her now." The look in her eyes and the way she said the words sent a chill through Casey. She sounded so reasonable, which he knew was just part of her act. He could pretty well guess what would happen if she was ever allowed access to Brianna. His daughter would be gone.

He held himself together, drawing on his police skills to keep from showing his anxiety. "Not this time," Casey told her evenly. "Every phone call, every conversation has been noted. Each time you just showed up on my doorstep has been sent to my lawyer. The fact that you disappeared for two years is the reason you won't ever have her. And as of now, you will not see her either. I've tried to be decent about this. But now I need to protect Brianna. I suggest you leave."

She put her elegantly manicured hands on her lips. "Or what?"

"I'll make a call to the police. You threatened me, and I have a witness. You might even spend some time in jail, if I'm lucky." He smiled grimly. "Now go. You do what you need to, but know I will do the same." He turned and waited for Vin in front of the house. They both went inside and closed the door hard against Alicia and anyone else would threaten him or his daughter.

"Do you really think that she'll file for custody?" Vin asked as Casey sat down to take off his shoes and socks and let his feet breathe.

"I don't know. Alicia tends to make threats when she thinks it will get her whatever it is she's fixated on in the moment. That I do know. But she doesn't stand a chance. Not after walking away for two years. In fact, it's likely the court will refuse to even hear her case. They've already ruled, so she'd have to appeal, and that would take a very long time." Casey sighed. "She isn't going to stay here all that long. There is nothing for her here other than Brianna. I don't understand why she wants her so badly. It's not like Brianna even likes her. My daughter is a very good judge of character. Brianna is wary of her mother but is trying to be nice."

Vin sat next to him and took his hand, entwining his fingers. "What can I do to help?"

"Nothing right now. Just being here helps immensely. Tomorrow I need to look into this Renaldo character. See what kind of person he is."

"How will you do that?" Vin asked.

"We know the kind of car he drives. We can do a thorough search on that, to start with. Carter was going to look into it for me, but we've been busy with this drug case, and I wasn't going to pull anyone away from it." He sighed. "Strictly speaking, it's not something I should be doing, but this whole situation strikes me as odd. And she's now threatened me and Bri."

"Let your friends help you," Vin told him gently. "Carter will do what's right, and so will Red and Donald. They want the same things you do. But don't put yourself or your career in jeopardy. That isn't going to help anyone." They sat still for a few minutes while Casey calmed down. "Let's get ready to go."

Casey went upstairs and got fresh socks. Once his feet were comfy and dry again, he and Vin left the house. Before he got in the car, he looked around for Alicia. She seemed to be gone, thank God. At least for now.

THE GUYS had already grabbed a table, and once Casey and Vin sat down, they ordered their beers and looked over the menu.

"I just got this from the system at work," Carter said, handing Casey his phone. "The Mercedes is a rental, but their agreement is with a Renaldo Madrigal. The address is in Philadelphia. But I checked it, and it's an empty lot. I couldn't find much on him— there is very little information available. But we know he is in the country on a Costa Rican passport. Other than that, all we know is that he seems shady and hard to pin down. So if we want to uncover anything else, we're going to have to do some digging. But there is one other thing that I found interesting…." Carter paused while the server brought their drinks. Casey could already feel his muscles tensing, and Vin patted his leg under the table, which helped.

"Casey, relax. You're here with friends," Vin whispered.

"Is there something we don't know?" Terry asked.

Casey shrugged and turned to Vin, who seemed to understand Casey was finding the situation hard to talk about. His emotions were swimming very close to the surface at the moment, especially where his daughter was concerned. "Alicia was waiting when we got back to the house. She says she's going to cause trouble."

"As I was saying, I came across an interesting fact. It seems that Renaldo Madrigal has close ties to the Lorez family. Which I believe is Alicia's family, right? The two have married across the aisle many times."

"So he is definitely someone she met back home," Casey added, and Carter nodded. "I'm trying to access more about the two families, but I'm running into some interference." That was what Carter already said when he ran into a wall of secrecy. "The impediment is the DEA."

Vin touched his leg. "Could it be?" Vin asked, and Casey shrugged. Sure, it was possible that two parts of his life were colliding, but he wasn't going to jump to conclusions. Stranger things had happened, and it wouldn't surprise him if Alicia had teamed up with Renaldo and his family to try to gain the advantage in her quest to get her daughter back. Renaldo seemed to have money, and maybe Alicia was hoping to acquire some influence that way. He wouldn't put anything past her at this point.

"All right, let's all have a drink," Donald said brightly. "To a successful walk and hopefully bringing this business to a conclusion." He raised a glass, and they all followed along. Casey pushed away his worries and took a swallow of his beer. Whatever Alicia decided to try next, he'd be ready for her.

CHAPTER 7

VIN WOKE up the following morning in Casey's bed. God, it would be so easy for him to get used to this.

Casey was sliding out from under the covers.

"You really are the earliest riser I know," Vin said, blinking at the clock. It wasn't yet six, and Casey seemed already raring to go.

Brianna was still at her grandmother's place. Casey's mom had called while they were at dinner and asked if Brianna could spend the night, and that meant that Casey and Vin had had the entire house to themselves. Consequently, Vin ached in all the right places, and as he moved, reminders of the prior evening's activities made themselves known.

"I need to get into the station," Casey said. "There are a few things I need to check up on. And maybe I'll even figure out who this Renaldo is." He leaned back over the bed, and Vin kissed him. "I wish I could stay here and spend the day with you. But I need to see if I can make some headway. And I should check with the state police to see if they learned anything more about the little farming operation we discovered."

Vin needed to get going as well. Still, it would have been nice to play hooky with Casey today. They were quickly running out of time.

Vin roused himself out of bed and began getting dressed. "I need to check on my dad, and…." He let his words trail off. The truth was, he really didn't have much to do.

"I should be finished about five. I'll pick up Brianna, and then maybe we can get together, if you want." Casey disappeared into the bathroom.

"You don't need to make room for me. I know you have a full life." Vin finished getting dressed. Going back to his dad's place was the right thing to do. The more he thought about it, the more this… thing… with Casey was starting to feel like playing house. "Besides, I have a few things that I need to do."

Casey swept back inside the room and right up to him. "You don't have to make shit up to impress me or… God knows what. I was suggesting that we get together for dinner because I like spending time with you." His eyes were so deep, almost black, and Vin thought he could get lost in them. "But if you don't want to have dinner with us, then just say so."

Vin could hear the hurt in his voice. "I do," he said, swallowing around the roughness that had set in. "It's stupid. I don't have much to do at all during the day. Dad and I can only talk about so much, and then I have to find some project or other to kill a few hours." He sighed. "I just didn't want you to think you had to invite me over because you thought I was bored and that…." Even his reasoning for acting like an ass sounded stupid.

"I wish we could spend the day together. But I can't—not today. I'm off tomorrow, though, and I arranged for a day on Friday. Being a cop means working some pretty irregular hours. But that doesn't mean we have to like them." Casey bent down and kissed him. "Do you want me to give you a ride to your dad's?"

Vin shook his head. "I'll go down and make some coffee. Then I can walk home. The fresh air will do me good." It would also give him a chance to clear his head. Vin needed to figure out why in the hell he was so turned around all of a sudden. Maybe there were just so many things to consider, and they were coming at him all at once. He liked being home and seeing his father again. Being able to spend time with his dad and getting to know him as an adult, not a kid, was pretty cool. His dad wasn't the same person Vin remembered when he was growing up.

The house and town felt more comfortable and familiar than he'd remembered too. It was as if he'd truly come home.

But LA was also home, and he'd built a life for himself there—one that was his alone, where he wasn't reliant on his family or anyone else. And he wasn't sure he wanted to give that up. He'd worked hard to build his reputation and stand on his own.

Besides, if the shop and greenhouse sold, would he want to see them change? They were one of his biggest connections to his mother. She had loved that place, loved making things grow. And she'd passed that love on to him.

God, Vin's head was swimming with all the possibilities. If he wanted to take the easy way out, he'd just go back to LA and let the chips fall where they may. But that would mean leaving Casey behind… and he'd just found him again.

Casey kissed him again, harder this time, and the answer to his question became painfully clear. The trouble was that he liked what was going on. Things with Casey felt right, even though they probably shouldn't have. Vin lightly stroked Casey's cheek and then he pulled away, standing up straight.

Vin got his shoes on and went downstairs to start the coffee maker and put a little distance between the two of them. Once coffee was ready, he poured some in a mug for each of them, then filled an extra to-go cup for Casey. They drank in silence. Vin didn't quite know what to say. Not that there was anything wrong with that sometimes. It was more like things felt right—too right for something that had an expiration date.

"Call me when you're done with work, and I'll stop by the store to get something for dinner. You and Brianna can come over to our place to eat. Dad would love the company."

Casey smirked, and Vin wondered if he could see right through him. "That would be nice. Should I bring a bottle of wine or something?"

"Perfect. Red." At least now he had an idea of what to cook. "I can do a beef roast with potatoes and carrots. It's my mother's recipe—I found it the other day in a kitchen drawer. And it's been a long time since I've had it." He forced away the gloom that threatened him. That was another reason he needed to go back to LA. Everything here—from the food to the house and the business—reminded him of his mother. Heck, even the ringing of the bells at the old courthouse made him stop, just to listen, the last time he was downtown, because his mother used to tell him stories about how when she was young, she'd known what time it was—and knew whether it was time to come home for dinner—because of those bells.

Vin expected the old pain to resurface, but it didn't. Yeah, there was still a small part of him that felt empty when he thought of his mom. But now he could also remember the good things—like her smile, and the way they'd walk around downtown at Christmas, looking in stores. She was also the first person to show him where a civil war shell had damaged one of the buildings.

"Sounds great. I remember your mom making that," Casey said. "I'll talk to you then."

"Can you let me know if you find out anything about the spot we found?" Vin asked, and Casey nodded, his phone chiming.

"My pal Wyatt was right. The state police took a couple of guys into custody—they appear to be local, growing the pot for their own use. A small-time operation. Still, Wyatt said they're going to keep the area under surveillance for a while longer, just in case." He shook his head. "I had hoped it would be something we could use, but it didn't pan out."

Vin heard the disappointment in his voice. But then, things didn't always work out the way you wanted them to. Vin knew that firsthand.

When Vin finished his coffee, he wound his arms around Casey's neck. He intended to kiss him lightly, but Casey set his mug aside, then pulled him into his arms and kissed him hard, pouring intensity and energy into the meeting of their lips. Then Casey backed away.

"Vincent Robins, I've known you for a long time. So don't think I'm not well aware that you want to walk because you need some time to think things over." He picked up his mug again.

"Then why the hotter-than-hell kiss?"

Casey leaned closer. "I wanted to give you something to think about," he whispered.

"HEY, DAD," Vin said as he walked into the house he'd grown up in. He found his father in the kitchen, making scrambled eggs. Vin had mulled things over on the walk home and had realized that there was no way for him to get *everything* he wanted. He was going to have to choose. And what shocked him was that he was starting to think that staying in Carlisle was something he might actually want to do.

"You hungry?" his dad asked, already opening the refrigerator door to pull out the carton. "I wasn't sure when you were going to be home." He cracked a few more eggs and added them to his mixture. "How was your visit?" He poured the eggs into the heated pan and continued working, then put a couple slices of bread in the toaster.

"It was good." Vin got out two glasses and poured them each some juice. "You know, I thought you might be uncomfortable about this."

His dad shook his head. "About what? You're an adult, and what you do is your business. Besides, you've usually made good decisions, and I have every confidence that you'll continue to do that." He stirred the eggs around in the pan and grabbed the toast when it popped and added a piece to each plate. "You know, son, sometimes the decisions we're faced with aren't the ones we thought we'd be making. Life throws us all curveballs. And it's how we deal with them that determines the course of our lives." He took the pan off the stove and divided the eggs between the plates.

"You're sounding really philosophical, Dad." Vin rolled his eyes and then dug into the food, his hunger kicking in as soon as the first bite hit his belly.

"I am not." He set down his fork. "I'm trying to tell you that I want you to think hard about what you're doing with Casey… and that little girl. And just so you know—and don't get all contrary on me—I'm happy that you're spending time with them. It's a good thing." He picked up his fork again. "All I want is for you to be happy. And to maybe consider that you could actually be happy here."

He lowered his gaze to his plate. "Yeah, I know that I just might have jinxed it by saying something, but there it is. True love, contentment, happiness—take your pick of whichever one you want to use—they all require hard decisions and sacrifice. But they're worth it. They were for your mother and me, and they will be for you too." He went back to eating. "And that's all I'm going to say on the subject."

Vin rolled his eyes and half growled to himself, because for his father, that was saying one hell of a lot. Not that Vin was surprised at his father's feelings—just that he actually chose to express them. Vin had always known his father loved him, but his dad hadn't ever been a demonstrative parent. That had been his mother. But now it looked as if that might have changed. "You said a mouthful, Dad."

"You're my son, and I know I was... distant when you were growing up. But that was what I was taught. 'Be a man, don't show emotion or express your feelings.'"

"What changed?" Vin asked.

"Losing your mother. Her death has left a hole in my life that will never be filled. I couldn't manage the loss—it was too big. You were here for a while, but then you went on to find a new life, and I had to rebuild mine. Only I did a horrible job of it—I didn't rebuild anything. I closed the business and then just put my life on hold, waiting for your mother to walk back through that door—something that was never going to happen. But you... you made a new life. You made plans and then did your best to make them happen."

"But they didn't. At least not yet. The business I wanted was for sale, but I couldn't come up with the money to buy it." Still, he was getting there. "I have a name out there, Dad, and I like LA. It's exciting."

"Then by all means, go back, if that's where you think your future is." He set his piece of toast aside. "Just think about what's out there for you, and what there is here. Then make your decision." He finished his toast and juice before taking his plate to the sink. Vin finished eating as well and then did the dishes, since his dad had cooked.

"Dad," he said, his hands in the dishwater, "what do you have planned for today?"

"Just watching television. And I'm thinking it's time I cut the grass again. You know your life is as boring as shit when you look forward the mowing the lawn."

"Then let's do something about it," Vin said. "Do you have any idea how long it's been since you and I did something together?" He tried to remember and couldn't.

His dad shrugged, but Vin pulled out his phone to see what was going on around town. Since it was midweek, there wasn't much. One thing he did know—Gettysburg was out of the question. And a walk downtown held no interest for him. Then he hit on something they could do. He checked the time and realized he could let his father putter around the house for a while. A short time later, Vin bundled his dad into the car for a trip to the tastiest place on earth.

"I can't believe we're going to Hershey. Your mom and I took you there when you were a kid."

"Exactly, and now I'm taking you. We'll go on the goofy chocolate ride, and I've called ahead so we can eat in the Circular at Hotel Hershey for lunch. I always wanted to do that, and now we can." He got on the highway and pointed the car to the east. Maybe it was time he got one part of his life in order.

"DID YOU really need to buy all that chocolate?" his dad asked as they headed home later that afternoon.

"I figure I'll save most of it for Casey and Brianna." He chuckled, and his dad grinned and reached for yet another peanut butter cup. They were his father's favorite, and Vin had gotten him a bag of his own. It looked like he intended to munch his way through the entire bag. "And you don't need all that sugar." Good Lord, now he sounded like his mother. From the smirk he received, his father was probably thinking that same thing.

"So this roast you say you want to make… did you notice the cooking time?" Dad asked, and Vin groaned. "I think you need to switch to plan B. I remember that stuff taking hours in the slow cooker."

"Okay. Then we'll stop at the store and figure something out." Steaks were just fine with him. And while he was there, he grabbed a package of chicken nuggets, just in case Brianna wanted them instead of steak.

"Look at you, getting ready to cook," his dad teased as they pushed the cart through the store. "You know, your mama always said she could tell

when a man was in love because he started cooking."
He grinned, and Vin rolled his eyes.

"Or maybe it's a sign that spending time with his
dad is about as exciting as watching paint dry." He
glared at his father, who just shook his head. "Come
on, I need some apples and stuff. I want to make a
Waldorf salad." Now that he had the meat and the
vegetables, he picked out a combination of sweet
and tart apples and added them to the cart. "I think
that's all we need."

"Well, between this and the car full of candy, I
think we have enough to make everyone happy." Dad
pushed the cart toward the cashier. Vin paid for the groceries; then he and his dad hauled them to the car.

When Vin pulled up in front of the house, the
Mercedes he'd seen outside Casey's house was
parked down the street. He pulled in and watched,
but no one got out.

"What are you looking for?" Dad asked, turning
to see what he was looking at.

"Maybe nothing," Vin answered and got out of the
car. He grabbed the groceries and headed inside, with
his dad following behind. Once in the kitchen, he got
things set out on the table for later. "What the hell?" he
whispered to himself when he saw Alicia and a man—
probably Renaldo—walking around the greenhouse.
Dad came in, and Vin headed out back. "Can I help
you?" he asked as he strode across the lawn.

"We were just looking," Alicia said, a little startled, which pleased Vin. "I understand it's for sale."
She peered at the sign.

"Yes, it is," he answered and pulled out his phone. He sent Casey a quick message that Alicia and a man he assumed was Renaldo were at the greenhouse, snooping around. He wasn't buying their cover story.

Renaldo quickly glanced around, but Alicia did the talking. "I wanted to talk to you about it." She stepped forward. "You've got yourself a nice place here. I can see that it was once something special. Maybe it can be again." Her eyes darted around, but it was Renaldo's stare that sent a chill up his spine. His eyes were black and flint-hard.

"Maybe." Renaldo was intimidating, but Alicia was cold. The combination was unnerving, but Vin did his best not to let his trepidation show. He lived in LA and worked with high-powered clients. If you showed weakness in any way, they ate you for lunch. "You stopped by for a reason. Somehow I doubt it was because you were interested in purchasing a florist business."

Alicia's upper lip curled slightly. "No. I have no interest in flowers, or the men who work with them."

"Then I suggest you go back to your car and leave. And take Mr. Madrigal with you." He was getting tired of these two. Vin saw a spark of annoyance pass over Renaldo's features. "In fact, maybe you should both just head on back to Costa Rica. You're a free woman. You can marry anyone you like and start a new life. So do that."

She took a small step forward, her perfect make-up and bloodred nails only accentuating the predator that looked back at him. "And I have a suggestion for you," Alicia whispered, her accent becoming more pronounced. "You need to stay away from him if you know what's good for you."

Vin was about to respond when a police car turned down the lane, heading in their direction. It pulled up and Red got out. "Is there a problem?"

"Not really. She's just making some threats, trying to scare me." Vin didn't look away from her for a second. There was menace in her that Vin didn't trust. What he didn't understand was whether Renaldo was the one in charge but let her do the talking, or if Alicia had some sort of agenda and Renaldo was simply helping her. The dynamic between them was a little confusing.

"Would you like to press charges?" Red asked him. "I can take a statement and bring them in." Red was intimidating on a good day, but pissed off the way he was right now, he was downright scary. Alicia paled slightly. Clearly she'd gone farther than she intended to.

"I just want them to stay away from me and my father," Vin said. While he could press charges, he didn't have any witnesses that Alicia had said what she did, and neither she nor Renaldo was likely to admit what they'd been doing.

"Then, ma'am, I think it's best if the two of you walk back to your car and leave." Red stood a little taller, which only increased the intimidation factor. Not that it worked perfectly, especially when Casey got out of the car and stood just behind and off to the side.

"You can't—" she started to argue, but Renaldo gently touched her arm, and she turned and stomped down the lane toward the house.

"Ma'am, I suggest you stay on the road." Red pointed back the way they'd come. "You're trespassing on private property, and I don't think you're welcome."

It looked as if she was contemplating going across the yard, regardless of Red's admonition, but then she returned to the tarmac and continued walking toward the main road.

"She is mad as hell," Casey whispered as he watched her go. "Damn, Red, you sure knew how to handle her."

Red nodded. "She's changed a lot since she left. Your ex-wife was always used to getting what she wanted, but now I think she's a bit obsessed." He cleared his throat. "I think she's going to come after you somehow, and it wouldn't surprise me if she used Vin to try to do it."

"Me?" Vin asked.

"Why do you think she was here? My guess is that Alicia wanted to check you out to see what kind of person you are. It's a lot easier to size someone up face-to-face." Red patted his shoulder. "But you gave her as good as you got."

"What I don't understand is why she's even interested in me. I've only met her a few times." This situation was getting out of hand. "I wish I knew what her goal is and what the heck Renaldo is doing. Today he acted a lot more like a bodyguard than anything else."

Casey leaned forward. "You think Alicia is the leader?" That clearly made him think. "She always knew what she wanted, and she'd push me to get it, but she never was the type to go and get it herself. She was more of a power-behind-the-throne kind of person. Maybe that's changed."

"Either way, that woman is scary," Red said.

"Both of them are," Vin interjected. "It's obvious that Alicia is mean-spirited, but Renaldo is something else. I've looked into his eyes—the man has no soul. It wouldn't surprise me if he turned on Alicia in the end." He shivered. "He gave me the creeps. Thanks for getting here as fast as you did."

"Glad you called," Casey said. "If you could, write up the gist of what you talked about, sign it, and date it. I'll pass it on to my lawyer. If Alicia is threatening people, especially those in my life, then she needs to be held accountable."

He nodded. "See you in a few hours?" He was so tempted to step closer and kiss him, but Casey was on duty.

"You bet. And don't hesitate to call if they show up again." Casey turned back toward the car, then stopped. "What were they doing out here, anyway?"

"Alicia said she'd heard the shop and greenhouse were for sale, so they wanted to take a look. But they didn't seem as if they were checking out real estate." He shook his head. "I was thinking… you might want to find out where she's staying. That might give you a lead on the BMW you're looking for." He nodded toward the greenhouse. "It was weird. They seemed to be looking for something, though I don't know what. They came from the other side of the greenhouse. I saw them turn the corner before they caught sight of me."

Red and Casey took a look around the property but didn't find anything. Maybe Alicia and Renaldo had really been interested in buying, but that idea didn't sit well with Vin. And if it wasn't that, what were they doing? He doubted that they'd come to see the greenhouse out of curiosity.

Once Casey and Red left, Vin headed back to the house.

"What was all that about?" his dad asked when he returned. "Who were those people?"

"The woman is Casey's ex-wife. She's a real piece of work." He wasn't going to use the word that came to mind, but it definitely fit.

"Never liked her. Who was the man?" His dad sipped his beer, and Vin wondered how many he'd had. There were two empty cans on the kitchen table.

Vin grabbed a soda and went to sit down on the sofa. "His name is Renaldo. But I don't know if he's her boyfriend, her bodyguard, or what. I get this weird vibe from him, though he's nearly impossible to read. Both of them are stone-cold." He drank, and when his father finished his beer, Vin brought him some water, cheese, and a few crackers. "We're having company for dinner." That last thing he wanted was for his father to overindulge.

"I remember," he grumbled, then ate the snack. Finally he settled in his chair, and Vin figured he'd doze off for a while.

Needing something to do, Vin left his dad to nap and went into the basement. Thankfully it was fairly clean, though the shelves his mom had used for years to store the jams, jellies, fruits, and vegetables she'd put up sat empty. He wandered toward the back and dug around in a few boxes. He smiled when he came across his mother's shears and snips. For years they'd sat on her worktable in the shop. He also found his mother's other supplies and what looked like a metal cash box. It was locked, but he could hear something moving inside, though it didn't jangle.

After putting some things aside to talk to his dad about, he carried the box upstairs and set it on the coffee table. "Any idea what this is, Dad?

"I found that in the shop when I was cleaning out your mother's things. I never came across the key, and I didn't have the heart to break it open to see what was inside. Maybe Casey can get into it. Police officers are good at getting past locks, I've heard."

"Where was it?" Vin asked.

"In the back room, under the shelf. Your mother always kept it there. I don't think she realized I knew about it. It was with her private things, and after she died, I brought it back here." He seemed barely able to look at the box. "There are times when everything reminds me of her."

Vin leaned forward, catching his dad's attention. "Have you ever thought of dating?"

His dad's eyes widened. "You want me to find another woman? Wouldn't that make you feel like I was trying to replace your mother?"

Vin shook his head. "No one ever could. But Dad, there's no reason for you to go through the rest of your life alone. If you don't want to date, that's your decision. But I won't hold you back." He just wanted his dad to be happy.

"There is someone I've gone out with a few times, just for coffee or dinner. She was in your mother's garden club, and we met again at a funeral a few months ago. Connie and I started talking, and then we went out for coffee. She lost her husband four years ago."

"Connie Vargas?" Vin asked. "You're seeing her?" He was both shocked and pleased. "Aren't you lucky. I remember her from when Mom would have the club over to the house. She brought the best snacks. One time she made ice cream cake."

"That was years ago," his dad said.

"Yeah, but it was memorable." He grinned. "If you and Connie are seeing each other, then that's great. I'm happy for you." It felt funny talking to his dad about dating. But after all, he'd brought it up. "Just as long as you're being safe and using protection." His dad sputtered, and Vin chuckled. "I don't want you bringing home any little surprises." God, he remembered the time he and his father had had that conversation back when he was about fourteen. "So sheath the weasel, Dad."

"That's enough," his father said through his laughter. "My weasel is just fine, and I don't think either one of us has to worry about a baby. If it does happen, our first call will be to CNN or the *National Enquirer*. Now, it's getting late. Don't you have someone coming over for dinner?" Yeah, his dad was changing the subject.

"Okay, I need to get busy. But don't you think you should invite Connie over while I'm here? And maybe see if she'll bring her flan?"

His dad groaned. "Sometimes I wonder where your smart mouth comes from, but then I remember how much you take after your mother."

"And with that, I'm going to start dinner."

"MR. VIN!" Brianna said excitedly as she hurried in the house. "Daddy and I made cookies." She handed him the plate. "And they're not Mommy's cookies." She made a face. "Daddy says we never have to make her butt cookies again."

"Thank you." He knelt and gave her a hug. "We're having steaks for dinner. Do you want that or chicken nuggets? I got both, just in case."

She bounced. "Chicken nuggets. Daddy doesn't like them, so I can't have them at home. He says they're processed junk food." The look she gave her father was priceless.

"Well," Vin grinned, "we can't let you get nugget-deprived." He was glad he'd made the right choice. He picked up the bag from their trip and put it on the entry table. "These are for when you go home. Mr. Mack and I went to Hershey today, and he went a little crazy in the store."

"Me? I wasn't going to buy anything."

"Says the guy who ate half a bag of peanut butter cups on the way home," Vin teased, and Casey grinned.

"I brought some of my dolls," Brianna said. "Is that okay? They get hungry too."

Vin smiled. "Of course." Then he got her set up in the living room under a blanket tent. She squealed that her dolls had never camped out before, then proceeded to play, handing out chores to each toy. He returned to the kitchen, while his dad stayed with Brianna and the television.

"You sure are great with her," Casey said as he slipped his arms around his waist. Vin closed his eyes for a second, enjoying the closeness. "She was talking the entire trip over here about Mr. Vin," Casey continued. "How you play LEGOs with her. But mostly I think it's because you listen to her." Vin leaned back. "Oh, and we found the BMW. It was in the borough parking structure. From what we could see, it had only been there for a couple days."

"Abandoned?" Vin asked, turning slightly. God, he could stay like this for hours.

"I suspect so. It's still there in case someone tries to retrieve it. We ran the plates and registration, but it's registered to someone who's been dead for a year. We're checking out relatives and such, but that will take some time. The state police are watching the farming operation, just in case more people are involved. But they've already got their guys, so it's not likely." Casey sighed.

"But on a nicer note," he continued, "Alicia and her… whatever Renaldo is… are leaving in a few days."

"How do you know?"

"Their visas have been called in—at least Renaldo's has. They have to go. I called a friend in Immigration, and they seemed quite determined to get him out of the country. So if Alicia goes with him, then that's one big problem solved for me. Let her live her life and leave us alone."

"I hope that's the case," Vin said, though he doubted it would be that easy. Alicia didn't seem the type to give up on something she wanted just because of a pesky phone call from Immigration Services.

Casey tightened his hold. "God, I hope so too."

Vin's phone vibrated with incoming messages, but he ignored it. This moment was too good to interrupt.

Brianna's laughter rang in from the other room. Casey's arms slipped away, and he went in to join the others in the living room, his rich, deep laughter blending with his daughter's. Vin peered in and smiled at the sight of the two of them on the sofa, Brianna on her dad's lap, fighting off Casey's attempts to tickle her.

His dad got up and walked into the kitchen. "You know, you're a fool if you choose to give that up without even trying to see if it could work," he said softly on his way to the refrigerator.

Vin was starting to think the same thing. Was his life in LA so great that he couldn't even consider other opportunities? He turned back to the kitchen and prepped the steaks for the grill, made the salad, and put the potatoes in the oven to bake. His phone vibrated again. He sighed and pulled it out of his pocket.

Reluctantly, he pressed the button to accept the call. "Hi, Sue, what's going on?"

"God, I need your help." The owner of the shop in LA sounded frantic. Sue was usually so calm and methodical. "I have two weddings and a celebrity brat birthday party to get ready for, and Louise walked out." She huffed. "I'm up to my ears in work, and I'm going to be here all night. I thought the business had sold, but it fell through and…." She really was at the end of her rope.

"I'm on the other side of the country," he said calmly, thankful he wasn't there. Sue had been in the business for more than three decades and knew everything there was to know. Louise had been one of her designers for ten years. Something bad must have happened for her to walk out. Still, it wasn't his problem. "I did the designs for the weddings, so you don't need to start from scratch. Just call in the people you have, and they can help you put together the arrangements. Do you need me to send them to you?"

"God, yes. I can't find them." She was starting to freak out. "What I really need is for you to come home and take over this place. We can be partners or something. We can work something out. But I'm getting too old for this." She sighed.

Vin spoke calmly to her as he used his father's computer to log in to the flower shop system. He found the designs he was looking for and sent them directly to her. Once that was done, he poked around until he found the plans for the party. Louise had put that together, and it took a little time, but he got those to Sue as well.

"There you are. That should make things a lot easier," Vin said, trying not to get too excited about what Sue had just suggested. She was stressed.

"I'm serious, Vin. When you get back, we'll figure out some sort of partnership agreement that works for both of us." She seemed calmer now that she had a way out of the mess she'd found herself in. "You're so good with the clients. They just love you." He heard her take a deep breath. "Let me call you Thursday and we can talk about it some more, if that's okay. It would give you something to come home to." Sue said goodbye and hung up, leaving Vin's head spinning. He could hardly believe it! Things never worked out the way he wanted them to. But it looked like this time, they just might.

Vin set down his phone, a little shell-shocked.

"Work?" Casey asked.

"Yeah. The owner needed some of the designs I did for a couple weddings and a birthday party." Vin tried not to think about Sue's offer. It was almost too good to be true.

"Birthday party? With flowers?" Casey asked.

"Oh, yeah. This one is for a six-year-old. Twenty-five little girls and their mothers. Arrangements for every table and balloon bouquets spread around the venue. All of it in various shades of pink and white. Of course, the flowers are for the mothers and the balloons for the kids. It's a huge affair at a country club in Bel Air. You'd think they could just let the six-year-olds have fun, but apparently one of the other mothers had a huge party for her daughter, so this mother has to keep up with the Joneses." He sighed just thinking about it. "People out there seem to have money to burn."

"But is it real?" Casey asked.

Vin shrugged. "Sometimes I have no idea what's real and what's not. Sometimes it feels as if the universe is playing tricks on me." He set the completed salad in the refrigerator and checked on the potatoes. They were almost done, so he put some chicken nuggets in to heat.

Vin started up the gas grill and then got the steaks out. Once the grill was cleaned and hot, he put on the steaks, seared both sides, and then turned down the heat to allow them to cook. Then he finished getting the rest of dinner ready.

THE MEAL and the evening afterward were perfect, at least as far as Vin was concerned. Brianna played with her dolls or watched television. Dad was tired and went up to his room, leaving him and Casey to sit side by side on the sofa and talk. Eventually Brianna climbed into her father's lap, leaned against him, and closed her eyes. Casey gently moved her to the love seat, and Vin got a blanket. She was out, and that left the two of them alone.

"I never realized just how nice it is to be able to sit and talk. Alicia and I…." Casey started to say something, then stopped. "I need to quit doing that. Things with her were difficult most of the time. She wasn't the type of person I could relax around. Everything seemed to be a challenge. We were happy, but it wasn't a 'comfortable in your skin' kind of happy." He put an arm around Vin's shoulders, drawing him in.

The kiss between them was hot, gentle, and easy, as if they'd been doing this all their lives. Vin could almost feel the tension flowing out of Casey, and that was amazing and unsettling at the same time. With each passing day, the time they had together was dwindling. And Vin realized just how hard it was going to be to leave, regardless of the opportunities for him in LA.

Vin opened his mouth to try to tell Casey about his phone call, but he just couldn't do it. Telling him would mean that this—the quiet and the contentment—would all end. He leaned his head against Casey's shoulder, closing his eyes and trying to relax.

Casey's phone vibrated between them. He ignored it, so Vin did the same. The phone stopped and then began to vibrate again almost immediately. Casey sighed and fished it out. "Hey, Red," he said softly. "What?" His voice held worry. "There's someone already on the way…. Okay… I have Brianna here with me. There should be no one inside." He tensed, and Vin sat up and met Casey's worried gaze. "Right, I'll wait to hear from you." He put the phone aside.

"What happened?"

"My neighbor called the police because he saw someone in my backyard. He thought they might be trying to break in. Red said a couple patrol cars are already on the way." He held his head.

"We should go." Vin got to his feet. "I'll ask Dad to stay with Brianna. We can be on our way in two minutes." He went upstairs. His father was asleep on top of the covers on his bed, the television still on. "Dad… Dad…," Vin said. He hated to wake him.

"What going on?"

"There's an issue at Casey's. We need to go. Can you go downstairs to be with Brianna? She's asleep on the love seat in the family room."

He sat up slowly and got off the bed. "I'll be right down. You two go take care of things. I've got your back." He motioned toward the door, and Vin descended the stairs and met Casey at the front door.

"I'll drive," Vin said, then unlocked his rental. In minutes, they were at Casey's place, where two police cars sat parked in front of the house. Casey got out and went to meet the police while Vin parked. Then he got out and walked back to join Casey.

"Sir, you need to stand back," an officer he didn't know said as Vin came up the sidewalk.

"Jerry, it's okay," Carter told his fellow officer, who let Vin pass.

"What's going on?" Vin asked.

"When was the last time you were at Casey's?"

Vin paused cautiously. "Yesterday or the day before. We sat outside over the weekend. Why?"

Carter shook his head but led Vin inside and up to where the chief of police stood as tense as hell. "Sir," Carter said, "this is Vincent Robins. He was with Casey a few days ago. He might be able to shed some light on what we think is happening."

"I'm Chief Briggs," the man said with absolute authority. "I understand that you and Casey have been spending a lot of time together and that you were in the yard recently."

"Yes. Casey and his daughter were having dinner with my father and me when he got the call tonight, so I brought him down here. Where *is* Casey?"

"He's speaking with another officer. This is serious. We received a call from a neighbor that someone might be trying to break in, and then ten minutes later, we got a tip that we should check out this address for contraband. When we arrived, we found some plants in the backyard that shouldn't be there."

Vin narrowed his gaze. "Are you referring to marijuana?" he asked plainly. Euphemisms were useless. "There were none out there when I was here. I'm a florist, and I know plants. I was also young and living in California. Need I say more? I know what it looks like and smells like, and there was nothing in the yard the other night. This seems like a pretty ham-fisted attempt to frame Casey." And dammit, he had a pretty good idea who was behind it. "You are aware that his ex-wife is in town and that she is giving him hell because she wants to take their daughter back with her to Costa Rica." This was really low, even for Alicia. Then again, he wondered if she was actually behind it or if Renaldo was stepping in to help. Either way, this situation sucked.

Chief Briggs relaxed. "Good. I didn't want to believe this of Casey. He's a good officer. But this will need to be investigated. I've already got Internal Affairs involved. They're on their way."

"And I suppose you have to contact the DA as well." The chief nodded. "Make sure everything is aboveboard, because she is going to claim a cover-up." Vin seethed, but at the moment, all he wanted to do was find Casey.

"It was sloppy, but you're right. The only way to clear him is to be transparent." His expression turned dour once again.

"Don't worry. I know what you have to do," Vin said. The chief was going to have to suspend Casey for the duration of the investigation. It was the proper thing to do. That was going to crush Casey, while Vin just wanted to crush someone else.

"Chief," Carter said, pulling Chief Briggs away. Vin stayed near the door but didn't try to go in until Red come out to get him.

"How is he?" Vin asked.

"Mad as hell. But this sort of shit happens from time to time. And we have procedures for handling it." Red moved closer. "It's obvious that the plants haven't been there long."

"Like a matter of minutes," Vin interjected.

Red met his gaze. "We'll gather everything and make sure all the files are updated. He'll be out in a little while, so take him back to your place for the night. Carter and I will make sure the house is locked up. Just make sure he has the support he needs."

Vin nodded, and Red went back inside. Casey came out, tension and anger rolling off him, but he said nothing until they reached the car.

"What the hell?" Casey groaned as soon as he closed the car door. "Did they think we weren't going to see through something like that?"

"Maybe. But now there is going to be a record of pot being found on your property, which a certain someone can now use against you." He gripped the wheel tightly. "How long will you be suspended?"

Casey paused. "Just a few days. The chief said that they will get this done quickly. It's obvious that the plants were put there to cause trouble. Now they just have to find out who might have done it."

Vin rolled his eyes. "That's obvious. Alicia, and by extension Renaldo, is looking for ammunition."

Casey shrugged. "It could also be someone who's afraid we're getting too close with the investigation. I'm sidelined for a few days, and that means that others will have to take over. I'm not sure. But it's best not to jump to any conclusions." He sat back. "But you're right. Alicia is the one with the most obvious motive."

Vin pulled out and took Casey back to the house. His dad was watching television. Brianna was still asleep and hadn't moved. "Come on. I'll take you upstairs and show you where the two of you can sleep." As much as he wanted to spend the night with Casey, Brianna was going to need someone familiar nearby when she woke up. Relieved that he had re-made the bed earlier in the day, he gave Brianna and Casey the room he had been using.

"Where will you be?" Casey asked.

Vin got a pillow and blanket from the linen closet. "I'll sleep on the sofa. It's wide enough." He could see Casey about to protest. "Just take your daughter to bed and we'll sort everything out in the morning." That was the first priority.

Casey went downstairs with him and gently lifted Brianna off the love seat. She went right into his arms. "Daddy…."

"We're going to stay here tonight and go home tomorrow morning. Just hold on and I'll take you upstairs. Mr. Vin and Mr. Mack will be here when you wake up in the morning." As he slowly went upstairs, Vin began making up the sofa. He used the bathroom downstairs to clean up, then turned out the lights and lay down.

Vin checked his phone for the time. It was after ten, but he was wide awake and staring at the ceiling. He thought about turning on the television but didn't want to risk waking anyone. Vin could remember how, when he was a kid, he'd lie in bed, straining to hear the television downstairs. He could never quite tell what his mom and dad were watching, but there was always just enough volume for him to know that they had something on… and it always drove him crazy.

Footsteps on the stairs pulled his attention as Casey joined him in the family room. "Is Brianna asleep?"

"For now. She woke when I put her into bed and asked a bunch of questions. I told her everything was all right and that Uncle Red was watching our house for us." Vin pulled his legs forward, allowing Casey to pass, then sit down. "What do I tell her?"

"As close to the truth as you think she can understand," Vin said. "Someone put something bad in the yard, and the police want to find out who did it. You're staying here so the police can do their job." It seemed pretty simple to him. But maybe that was because

Brianna wasn't his daughter. It was always easy to give advice when it wasn't your decision to make. "I think the biggest thing is for you to be there for her."

"I wish Alicia had been," Casey said. "She keeps asking if I think her mommy loves her." He lowered his gaze. "How the hell do I answer that? How do I tell a little girl that I don't know if her mommy gives a damn about anybody?" His voice broke. "With the way Alicia's acting now, I don't know how she's feeling… or what she's thinking."

"She's furious and hurt," Vin said. "That's all there seems to be. Maybe she's angry at herself for the decisions she made. Or whatever. But her anger is directed at you, and that's what we should be worrying about. She could easily have done this."

"The neighbor says he thought he saw a man," Casey added softly. "Renaldo is a possibility."

Vin rolled his eyes. "Can you see Renaldo digging in the dirt?" He put his hand over his mouth. "He strikes me as the kind of man who would get others to do his dirty work. His hands were way too clean. Hell, the guy even has a manicure." He smirked and wriggled his fingers to show Casey his nails. "Hopefully whoever is behind it was careless and left something behind for the police to find." He paused, then looked over at Casey. "You know that if Alicia takes you to court, she'll use tonight's incident to cast doubt on your character."

Casey seemed less haggard than he'd been in the car. "I have no doubt. But I had nothing to do with it, and the chief, not to mention the other cops, will be able to attest to that. Alicia can yell all she wants, but she won't get anywhere. This is a distraction, nothing more."

"I know. The yard is too open to hide something like that for very long. And I told the chief that I'd just been in your yard the other day. So yeah, you're in the clear. But that doesn't mean it won't be brought up in a possible custody battle."

Casey nodded. "I'll send a note to the lawyer explaining what's going on. Heather is really sharp, and she'll be able to turn this against them." He seemed remarkably calm. "It's the fact that someone came after me specifically that has me worried. This is personal, and I'm worried I won't be able to keep Brianna safe. Red said that my neighbor thought that they might have tried to get in the house. From what I saw, it didn't seem like it. But…."

"You're a good officer and a good father. Brianna is lucky to have you." Vin shifted closer. "You can't let some asshole make you question everything you do. These people are crazy. I mean, how stupid is it to break into a cop's backyard and plant evidence? Really? Anyone could see through that in a heartbeat."

"Then why do it?" Casey asked. "The obvious answer is to get my eyes off of something else. It could be Alicia trying to discredit me, but for some reason I don't think so. She's more devious than that. She'd know we'd suspect her first thing… and so would the rest of the department."

"You know, maybe our friendly neighborhood drug distributor is starting to feel the heat and is hoping to put you out of action for a while. Maybe they want to get the department looking at you... instead of them." Vin shrugged, thinking out loud.

"I don't know. It wasn't like we were getting all that close to them. And why me, personally?" He sighed. "I wish I had some idea what was really going on."

"You'll put the picture together. You're just missing a few pieces." He took Casey's hand. "I'm just glad that you and Brianna were at my place."

"Why?"

"Because who knows how far these people are willing to go? If they're desperate enough to try to get you off the force, even if just for a while...." He didn't want to think about what else they might try. And what if they used violence next time? He shivered.

"It's going to be okay. The chief is handling this personally, and I've got the next few days off with pay. I'm not supposed to be investigating anything, so it looks like I'm going to have some time on my hands." He smiled slightly. "Can we talk about something else?"

"Of course," Vin agreed.

"Okay. So, I know your mom was the one who got you interested in working with flowers. But is that what you always wanted to do?" Casey asked.

Vin snickered. "I didn't at first. After all those years working in the shop, I really wanted to do something else. I went to college and thought I might try architecture, which didn't work out. I graduated with a degree in design and took the job I could get. My first job was to design the plantings and gardens for a gardening maintenance firm. I did a great job, and they kept asking me to do that work. Then the economy went south, and I was out of a job, all by myself on the other side of the country. Then I got the job with Sue because I needed the work and I knew I could do it. My design expertise came into play when the clients wanted something special. I guess I was destined for this."

"Okay," Casey agreed. "I'm following you."

"There was this wedding. The bride's really famous, and she'd seen some of my work at an expo and asked if I could make some of her arrangements. She wanted flowers hanging from the ceiling on invisible cords above each table. It would look like the arrangements were floating. So I came up with a way to make that happen for her. Then suddenly we were getting jobs for floral mobiles, sculptural pieces… you name it. Sue is a gifted florist, but I'm the one with the ability to make these complex pieces a reality. I design them for Sue, and then the florists get to work bringing my creations to life. With my help, of course." He pulled out his phone and flipped through the pictures. "This is one of the floating arrangements. In the low light they used for the evening, the filaments I used completely disappeared." He continued showing Casey his designs.

"Good God. How tall were those?"

"In total, ten feet. The candles alone are two feet high, and the arrangements are eight feet. There were four of them behind the head table."

Casey whistled. "How much does something like that cost?"

"Five thousand dollars each. We had to have the holders specifically constructed. Once the event was over, I worked with a company to electrify the pieces, and they were installed around the couple's pool. The cut-flower basins are now used as planters. They're stunning pieces and unique to them." Vin put his phone aside. "I like doing things like that. But…." He shrugged. "It gets to be a bit much after a while. The pressure to constantly perform at the highest level is intense. I love the creative part of the business—it's the people who sometimes drive me out of my mind. They want what they want, and they want it now. Granted, a lot are willing to pay for that. But constantly being under the gun is tiring. I think just once, I'd like to be able to design something for myself."

Casey shifted closer on the sofa. "And what would that be? When you get married? What flowers would you have? Would the display be ten feet tall?"

Vin chuckled. "No. I like fall colors. So, displays of mums and daisies with some sunflowers. Nothing too fancy, but lots of color. I'd even pick some fresh leaves and wind them into the decoration to add texture. I do love roses, but they're… well… roses. And everyone has them. Though I'd probably add red and yellow ones, just for some additional interest. The groomsmen would be in black tuxedos with bright flowers, and instead of bouquets, there'd be sprays of flowers up front on either side. Most brides love the spring or summer colors, but I'm a fall type of person I guess."

"What about something tropical?" Casey asked.

Vin grew excited. "I'd love a destination wedding. Caribbean, bright colors, getting married barefoot on the beach in casual clothes that billow just a little. Flowers from the islands everywhere." He chuckled half to himself. "I once did a wedding in Malibu where all the flowers were shipped in from Jamaica, and I did my best make everyone feel like they'd been transported to the islands. It was magical." He remembered how strange the idea had seemed, but once it was done, the effect had been stunning. A destination wedding without leaving home. "What about you?"

"I don't know. Alicia picked out everything for our wedding. If I was to get married again, I think I'd like to do it in the yard and fill the entire space with as much color as I could. I'd plant perennials so that the color would come back year after year. I love flowers, but I haven't had a chance to do much with the yard. Alicia wasn't interested—she hated doing anything outdoors." He shrugged. "Now that the house is mine, I'm thinking of changing a few things."

"Maybe I could help you. If you want, I could draw up some plans that you could use." He'd love to do that for Casey. "We could do some shrubs as a background and anchor, then add perennials and a few bulbs and annual beds so the yard will have color all season long." That sounded wonderful.

"Daddy," Brianna said softly as she shuffled into the room. She climbed into Casey's lap. "I woke up and you were gone."

"Were you scared?" he asked.

She shook her head. "I heard you talking."

"I see. Do you want me to take you upstairs?" Casey asked.

Brianna burrowed against him. She obviously wanted to be with her daddy. "Will we be able to go home tomorrow?"

"Yes, we will. But for now, we're having a sleepover at Mr. Vin's and Mr. Mack's. Is that okay?" She nodded. "Good. Go back upstairs and go to bed. I'll be up soon, I promise."

"I'm thirsty," Brianna said softly, trying to stay awake.

Vin got up and brought her a glass of water. Once she had a drink, she handed him back the glass with a smile and then went back up the stairs.

"I should check on her," Casey said, getting up to follow her.

Vin turned out the light and lay back down. He doubted Casey would return tonight. He understood that Brianna had to be his main focus. Still, it had been nice to have all of Casey's attention for a while.

"Vin," Casey said softly, and he sat up. Casey came over to the sofa and sat down next to him. "She's out like a light."

"There's been a lot of upheaval for her in the past week," Vin said. "I don't want to add to that."

Casey smoothed his hand over Vin's forehead, brushing the hair away. "Change is inevitable, and kids take it a lot better than we adults do." He stretched out, lying half on top of him. Vin loved the weight and tugged Casey down into a kiss.

"I keep thinking about the end of the week," Vin admitted, though as Casey kissed him again, the words dissipated in a haze of passion. God, what Casey did to him in just a few seconds. It was like he knew exactly how to light and feed the flame that simmered inside. Vin wound his arms around Casey's neck. With each touch, Vin knew he was getting closer to Casey. And it wasn't just that Casey's weight was currently pressing him against the cushions. His heart wanted this too, and it was so easy to just go along with it.

"Casey…," Vin paused, cupping his jawline in his hands. "You're making this so hard."

He smiled. "I think that's the point." He wriggled his hips, and Vin groaned.

"You know what I mean," Vin protested.

Casey stilled. "I do, and maybe that's my plan." He held Vin's gaze, drawing him in, crumbling Vin's resistance in seconds. "Sometimes you just have to take what you can get." Casey's voice was rough and barely audible, but that didn't matter. "There are times when we have to make the most of what we have and not think about what it'll be like when it's gone." He drew closer. "If I only get you for a short time, then I'm going to enjoy every minute of it."

Vin closed the distance between them, knowing that Casey was right but that going home at the end of the week was going to take more strength than he thought he had. And maybe that was the point. Walking away from someone you love should never, ever be easy. It should always leave a mark on your heart. And Vin was sure that by the end of the week, his was going to be marked up something good.

CHAPTER 8

CASEY WAS as quiet as possible when he returned upstairs, but apparently he wasn't as stealthy as he'd hoped. Mack came out of his room in a pair of green striped pajamas.

"Don't get old if you can help it," he said, imparting the wisdom of the ages. "Nothing seems to work right." He shuffled down to the bathroom, passing him. "Are you just coming up?"

Casey nodded. "Brianna is asleep, and Vin and I were talking."

Mack's knowing grin told Casey quite a bit. "Is that what they're calling it nowadays? Talking?" He took another step before pausing. "I'm happy… about you and Vin."

"He's only here for a week. I know that." He tried to keep the disappointment out of his voice but knew he hadn't managed it. "It's…." There was no need to go into all the complications, especially with Vin's father.

"I know what it is. I felt that once too. And I know what it's like to lose it," he said. "Fight for it. That's all I can tell you. Don't give up. Whatever happiness this life brings, hold on to it with both hands and don't ever let go. You'll regret it forever otherwise." And like a sage who had delivered his message, Mack continued on, closing the bathroom door behind him.

Casey went into the room he and Brianna were using and climbed into bed. Brianna lay on her side, her hands under her head. She didn't move as he settled on the mattress and tried to go to sleep.

He was exhausted, and his body wanted to just let go, but his head had other ideas. Vin occupied his mind in a way that no one else ever had. After just a few days together, Casey's life felt fuller, richer. Before, Brianna had been the light of his life—and she still was, but now, with Vin, there was color everywhere. He wasn't sure how he'd ever go back to a world filled with gray. But somehow he'd have to. Unless….

Maybe Mack was right. Maybe he had to try harder. Maybe he needed to show Vin what it would be like if he stayed. He'd give LA a run for its money. After all, the City of Angels might have movie stars and opportunity… but he and Brianna, Mack, and the people of this town weren't there. He just had to get Vin to see, somehow, that he had family and friends here… and love.

And he only had about four days to make it happen, so there wasn't a lot of time to waste.

He closed his eyes, trying not to think, but the wheels of his mind kept turning. Finally, after what seemed like hours, he fell asleep.

"Daddy," Brianna said, poking his arm.

Casey kept his eyes closed and pretended he hadn't heard her. It seemed like he'd just closed his eyes.

"I gotta go potty."

Casey forced his eyes open, got out of bed, and checked his phone. "It's six in the morning." He took her by the hand and led her to the bathroom, letting her go by herself. Once she came out, she headed for the stairs. "It's too early to go downstairs. Mr. Vin and Mr. Mack are still sleeping." He guided Brianna back to bed. "I promise you aren't going to miss anything fun."

"But Daddy, I'm not sleepy."

"But I am. So lie down and try to be quiet." Hopefully she'd go back to sleep. Lord knows he needed a few more hours.

Casey closed his eyes, and sleep almost instantly overtook him. The next thing he knew, the sun was streaming though the bedroom window and he was alone in the bed.

Casey jumped up and pulled on his pants, then grabbed his shirt and headed downstairs. "Those look really good," Brianna said from the kitchen. "Grandma always adds extra blueberries." Apparently his daughter was giving Vin instructions on making blueberry pancakes. "That's it."

"Now do I cook them?" Vin asked.

"Yes. But don't get the pan too hot. It takes time to make the pancakes fluffy." It seemed Brianna was an expert.

"Let Mr. Vin make his pancakes," Casey said, swooping in to tickle her.

She giggled but put her hands on her hips as soon as he stopped. "He has to do it right. Grandma's pancakes are special." She wasn't going to be put off. "That's right," she said when she returned her attention to what Vin was doing. "I think you got it."

Casey managed to stop himself from laughing, and Vin focused on his task, obviously trying not to chuckle as well.

Then Mack came in. "Let's set the table so we can eat while they're still hot." He took Brianna's hand, and they went into the other room.

Casey moved close to Vin and got a quick kiss.

"She's pretty amazing. I let her guide me, and she knew exactly what to do."

Casey shook his head. "My daughter can be a little bossy at times."

Vin shrugged. "I think she's just confident in what she knows. Obviously she and your mother have made these often enough that she knows how to do it." He flipped the perfectly golden-brown pancake. "She's smart, and she picks up on things quickly."

Casey rested his head against Vin's back. "Sometimes I wonder if she's too smart. She sees everything. And I worry that she sees the lies behind her mother's words. It makes me angry that Alicia cares so little, and that Brianna can see it." He stepped back when Brianna came in to see how Vin was doing with the pancakes.

"That's how Grandma's look. Good job," she said.

Vin added more batter to the pan, then put the finished pancakes into the oven to keep warm.

"There's butter and syrup in the refrigerator, along with juice. These are cooking pretty quickly." Vin kept an eye on the pancakes, ready to flip them when the moment was perfect, while Casey helped Brianna get the rest of breakfast ready. Casey poured the juice, and by the time everything was set at the table, Vin brought in a platter filled with pancakes. They looked heavenly. Mack and Brianna fixed their plates, and then Vin gave Casey a crack at the pancakes before he filled his own plate.

"These are really good."

"As good as Grandma's?" Casey asked, and Brianna grinned. "We just won't tell her, okay?"

Brianna nodded. "That would be bad."

Definitely. His mother could be a real pain in the butt, but her cooking was something she took deep pride in. She wouldn't be happy to have her role as the queen of her granddaughter's pancakes usurped.

Brianna ate her fill and drank her juice before asking to leave the table to play with her dolls.

"She seems comfortable here," Vin said. "That's good. Remember when you and I turned the basement into a roller rink?"

Casey nodded. They had both been given inline skates for Christmas one year, and since it had been so cold outside, they'd decided to skate in the basement. "We had so much fun down there."

"Until you almost tipped over Helen's preserve shelves. Then she put a stop to it and you two had to wait until spring. After that, the sidewalks weren't safe for anyone," Mack said with a smile. "This house has seen a lot of joy over the years. But lately…."

"I know, Dad."

Casey finished his breakfast and gathered up the dishes to take to the kitchen. "Brianna and I need to get out of your hair and back to the house." When his phone vibrated, he pulled it out and read Red's massage. He sighed and ground his teeth. Apparently Red and Carter had been asked to join the state police in a raid on the marijuana farm. Though they had a couple of locals in custody, the police had reason to suspect there were others involved. It was likely that they'd just find more locals, but still, Casey would have liked to have been able to go. But after yesterday's plant incident, it was out of the question. He'd been sidelined.

"Is something wrong?" Vin asked, watching him intently.

Casey shook his head. "It's from Red. They're raiding the farm we found, hoping that if there is anyone else involved, they'll be flushed out. He and Carter are going too. He says he'll let me know what happens."

"And you want to be there. Of course you do," Vin said. "Well, maybe we can find something else to do. We could walk to the park, or go downtown and see what's happening there. Get out of the house for a while."

Casey liked the idea of not sitting around ruminating all day on what he was being left out of. "We can do that. But Brianna and I need to go home first so we can change into clean clothes." Their overnight adventure hadn't been planned, so they hadn't even had a chance to grab a toothbrush. "Why don't we meet you back here in an hour, then?"

Vin and Mack agreed, and Casey took Brianna out to the car.

"I like Mr. Vin," Brianna said as he buckled her seat belt. "I saw you kissing him. Are you and Mr. Vin going to get married? Is he the reason you don't love Mommy anymore?"

Man, she could come up with the hard questions. "Mr. Vin and I like each other, but I don't know what's going to happen. And no, Mr. Vin has nothing to do with how I feel about your mother. Did she say something?" he asked as he pulled away from the curb and headed for home.

"Mommy says that you like boys and that's why you don't want her anymore. She said that you are a 'bominable nation."

"And what do you think?" Casey asked, cringing but knowing Brianna well enough that she would have her own ideas.

"I like Mr. Vin. He's nice. And Mommy left a long time ago. Mr. Vin was just here." She shrugged. "Maybe Mommy's mad because you don't love her anymore. But I know she doesn't love you. She says mean things about you. If she loved you, she would be nice."

Casey couldn't argue with that. "Is she nice to you?"

Brianna shrugged, which Casey thought was interesting. "She smiles, but she isn't really nice."

Damn, his daughter was more perceptive than he'd thought. "Will you marry a girl next time so I can have another mommy? Or will you marry a boy?" This was obviously something she was curious about if she was bringing it up again.

Casey tried to figure out how to tell Brianna the truth in a way she could understand. "Some people like boys, and some people like girls. That's just how they're made. I know girls who like girls, and that's okay. Some boys like other boys. Some people like both boys and girls."

"Is that what you are? Because you married Mommy and now you like Mr. Vin?"

"Yes. Is that okay?" Casey asked.

Brianna nodded. "Of course it is. Silly Daddy." She giggled. "Do I have to take a bath when we get home?"

"You can take one tonight. But how about you put on fresh clothes, wash your face and hands, and then brush your teeth, okay? Mr. Vin and Mr. Mack will be coming over, and we want to be ready."

When he pulled up to the house, he saw he had a visitor. Casey parked behind his mother's car, wondering what she was doing here. Once they were out, he went inside and found her sitting in the kitchen with a cup of coffee.

"I was wondering when you were going to get home. I heard from a friend that you've been suspended." Disapproval rolled off her.

Casey ignored her and turned to Brianna. "Go on upstairs and clean up while I talk to your grandma." He remained calm until Brianna was out of earshot.

"First thing, someone planted something illegal in my yard. The neighbor called the police just before they received an anonymous tip. No, the plants weren't mine, and the chief believes me. But an investigation must be done, so I'm on paid leave. Everyone at the station knows it's BS, but procedures have to be followed. So I stayed with Vin and his father last night and allowed the police to do what they needed to do here." He poured his own mug of coffee. "So all that disapproval that's rolling off you? You can stop it right now. There's no reason for it."

"Other than you're seeing Vin as more than just a friend. Alicia is upset about it, and she's Brianna's mother and has a right to see her daughter." His mother had certainly seemed to have changed her tune. "When she came to see me, I—"

Casey cut her off. "Alicia came to see you? And you're here to plead her case? You have to be kidding me. She left two years ago, shows up again, and suddenly you're best friends?"

"She just wants you, her, and Brianna to be a family again." His mother had really bought into whatever Alicia was selling.

Casey seethed inside, and it took all his willpower not to throw his mother out of the house. "Let me be clear—every word out of her mouth is a lie. The first thing Alicia asked me was how soon she could take Brianna to Costa Rica. She'd take her away from me, and from you too. You do realize, don't you, that if that happens, you will never, ever see her again? I don't know what game Alicia is playing, but you stepped right into it, and she's made you look like a fool. She isn't the same person. There's something dark inside her—even Brianna has picked up on it." He took a deep breath and tried to calm down, especially when he noticed her hand shaking as she put her coffee mug down on the table.

"You don't mean that," she said. "Alicia seemed fine to me."

"Well, she's not fine. She's dangerous. How can you take someone else's side over mine, especially when it comes to your granddaughter? I'm *your* son." He paused for a moment, letting that sink in. "Alicia gave up her rights when she left, and the courts made sure of it. All this disruption is going to end. I will protect Brianna with everything I have—even if it's against her mother. Now, can I trust you to look after Brianna, or do I need to find someone else to watch her?" Casey knew that this line of questioning would rattle his mother, but it was necessary. Whatever Alicia had told his mother had given her ideas that were wrong.

"Of course you can." She tried to sound offended, but it was fake, and they both knew it. "But she seemed so…." She lowered her gaze.

"I know, Mom. She seemed so nice, and she told you what you wanted to hear. When she came to see you, was Renaldo with her?" She seemed confused. "She's been with that man every time I've seen her. I'm not sure who he is to her, but she isn't one to play the 'hurt, alone, and innocent' card."

"But… things would be better if…," she said, then stopped. Casey just glared at her, his hands on his hips. "I have the right to my opinion."

"That may be true, Mom. But I don't have to listen to it, and neither does my daughter. I think I'm going to find someone else to look after Brianna. I don't know if I can trust you to keep my daughter safe." He turned away as Brianna came back down the stairs.

"Casey!" He could hear the hurt in her voice.

He paused, then let out a long breath. "Okay, you can look after her. But you will have to do as I ask as far as Brianna is concerned. Alicia is not to see her unless I'm there, and if she comes by, you have to turn her away. Period. I don't want you letting her in for a visit, or to have coffee and talk. Not while Brianna is there." He hurried over to his daughter and scooped her up. "Come say hi to Grandma." He squeezed her and put her down.

Brianna ran over to her grandmother for a hug. "Guess what? We made your pancakes this morning. Mr. Vin helped. They were good, but not as good as yours." Maybe Brianna was destined for a career in politics.

"What do you want to do today?" she asked Brianna.

"Daddy and Mr. Vin are going to take me to the park. Mr. Mack is gonna come too. I'm going to play and feed the ducks. Maybe we'll even see some dogs there." She sighed and looked up at Casey with wide eyes. "I love dogs. I wish I had one."

Casey shook his head. "Nice try, Bri."

Not discouraged, Brianna turned back to her grandmother. "I think we're going downtown for lunch, but I'm not sure. Do you want to come with us?" she asked.

"Yeah, Mom. Come along." Maybe seeing Vin again would make things easier for her. "You remember Vin from when we were kids." This could be a good thing. "Go finish up," he said to his daughter. "We'll leave in about ten minutes."

When Brianna raced off, he turned to his mother. "So… will you come?"

She lowered her gaze. "I don't know. I'm not sure what to think about you being with a man. Not even Vin. He was always a nice boy, and you were good friends. Is it serious between you?"

Casey shrugged. "Mom, I don't know what's going to happen, okay? Vin is supposed to go home on Sunday, and I may never see him again. I know he cares for me, but… I can't just ask him to stay if he doesn't want to. And we've only been seeing each other a few days. Maybe nothing will come of it and we'll both look back on this as a vacation thing. I'm trying not to analyze it too closely, because if I do, everything falls apart."

"But Brianna…."

Casey grinned. "She likes him. They made pancakes together this morning, and he plays LEGOs with her and even dolls, sometimes. It's wonderful to see them together. And Brianna loves Mack. You remember him. You and Helen were close friends."

She nodded. "I miss her."

His mother seemed willing to listen, so he took the opportunity. "I know you love Brianna and me. But please be careful. Alicia has an agenda, and I don't know what it is yet. She's become very selfish."

His mother finished her coffee and sighed. "But as a mother…."

Casey had almost been waiting for that sentiment. "Yeah, I know. You're a mother. But would you ever have abandoned me? Left the country for years and ignored me? And Dad?" That was the crux of the issue as far as Casey was concerned. He waited while his mother shook her head and reached for a napkin. "Just remember what she did. It hurt both of us. You remember how for months, Brianna would ask where Alicia was? I don't want that to happen again. And I'm afraid that Alicia's going to try to take Brianna back with her to Costa Rica somehow."

"You're serious," she whispered. "You really think she'd do that?"

Casey shrugged. "I have no idea what this Alicia is capable of. She was always strong-willed. But now she's… she seems to think that she has a right to whatever she wants." He watched as his mom wiped her eyes. "I need your support, Mom. No matter what happens. Okay?"

She nodded. "I've only ever wanted you to be happy."

"I know that. But this time around, I think the road to happiness is about as twisted and curved as Lombard Street, and I have no idea if I can see the end or just another bend."

"Then why take the chance?" she asked. "You know he's leaving in a few days. Aren't you just setting yourself up to be hurt?" She patted his hand.

"I probably am, Mom. But I think I'd rather experience some hurt for a while than not feel the way I do now. He makes my heart soar. The guys all like him, and he's had my back when I've needed him. When Alicia showed up, he was by my side, and when someone put pot in my backyard, he made sure Brianna and I were taken care of. Most people would take one look at me—a guy with a daughter and a past that's completely messed up—and run the other way. But Vin ran toward us. At least he has for now, so that's what I'm trying to do. Just live in the now." It was the best he could come up with.

"Okay," she said, which was a surprise. Then she stood. "I think I need to go. The garden club is meeting to work on the garden in the park. So I'll probably see you there at some point." She hugged him. "I just want you to be happy and for your road in this life to be as smooth as possible." She paused, and when Brianna came back, his mother sent her back upstairs on an errand to get her out of the room. "Listen to me. I saw the way you and Vin looked at each other when you were boys. It scared me. I saw that he cared for you and you felt exactly the same. Two boys making moon eyes at each other. The only blessing was that neither of you understood what was happening. Over time, life did what it usually does and pulled you both in separate directions. Then you met Alicia and seemed happy with her. I was so relieved, because I thought that meant you had left boys behind."

"Mom, I've figured out that I like both men and women. Brianna and I have talked about it in a very rudimentary way. She understands, and she likes Vin."

She nodded. "And how will she feel when he goes back to California?"

"She'll miss him, but she'll go on. Just like she will when Alicia goes back to Costa Rica. Brianna isn't made of glass, and neither am I. We're strong. Things may hurt, but we'll move forward and deal with it." It was the only answer he had. "Now, please come with us to the park. You can meet your garden club ladies there. But spend time with Vin and his father… and me."

She raised her eyebrows. "What are you doing?"

"It's simple. I want Vin to stay. I don't know how I can make that happen, but I'm going to give it my very best shot. I can't ask him—it has to be his decision—but…."

She sighed. "You're playing a game that I don't think you can win. But I'll come along with you, if that's what you want."

"Wonderful." He felt like he and his mom had actually connected. It had been a long time coming.

"Maybe you could invite everyone over for dinner on Saturday. It would give your father a chance to see Mack again. And it's nice to be included in your life."

"That's a great idea. Let's talk about it at the park," Casey said as Brianna came back down. "Do you remember where the cooler is?"

Brianna nodded and hurried off. Casey pulled water bottles and juice boxes from the refrigerator. Then he asked his mom to pack up the drinks while he headed upstairs to clean up quickly and put on fresh clothes.

"You ready to go?" he asked Brianna when he returned downstairs. "Grandma is going to join us."

"Yay!" Brianna took her hand as Casey gathered up everything they'd need. Then he locked up and they all walked out to the car. It was going to be a good day.

"MR. VIN, Grandma is going to come with us," Brianna said. She'd jumped out of the car and raced up to where he sat on the porch. The way she was acting, anyone would have guessed that it had been weeks since she'd seen him instead of an hour.

"That's nice." He knelt down and gave her a hug.

"We brought drinks too," she announced. "Is Mr. Mack ready?"

"He's getting you some corn for the ducks, and then we can go." Vin grinned, and Mack joined them on the porch. He greeted Casey's mother with a smile. "Clair, it's been too long." There was pain in his eyes for a second, but it passed quickly.

"I know." She smiled. "I miss her too." And just like that, the sun came back out in Mack's eyes. "But we all have to move forward, I suppose, and it's always nice to see old friends."

Casey picked up the cooler. "Are we ready to go?"

Mack handed Brianna her bag of corn for the ducks, and Brianna took the lead, half skipping ahead in anticipation.

"Don't cross the street without us," her grandmother called out.

"I won't," Brianna promised and hurried farther ahead. She was clearly excited and full of energy. Casey held the cooler and walked next to Vin, sharing a smile, their hands brushing more than accidentally while his mother and Mack caught up.

"She was waiting for us," Casey explained. "It seems Alicia has been talking to her. But I think she and I were finally able to clear the air." At least he hoped so. "How are things with your dad?"

Vin shrugged. "As good as can be expected. He wants me to stay, and he isn't beating around the bush. He wants me to come back and reopen the shop."

"Is that such a terrible idea?" Casey asked. "You would have something that's yours, and you'd be working for yourself. Once people saw what you were capable of, they'd flock to your work. I know it."

Vin skipped a step and nearly tripped, but caught his balance in time. "Sue called me the other day. She said she misses me. The sale she was hoping for fell through, and she's offering me a partnership in the business."

"I see." Casey had a ton of questions that he wanted to ask Vin, but he kept them to himself. The cop in him wanted to know why. Did the sale fall through because the shop wasn't as profitable as it appeared? If she was doing so well, then why sell? It wasn't his place to question it, and he knew he should be happy for Vin because it was what Vin had really wanted. "Are you excited about going back?"

Vin didn't answer right away. "There's some pretty amazing work waiting for me there. But I don't want to disappoint my dad. He really has his heart set on me reopening the florist shop, and…."

Casey took a deep breath. "All I'm going to say is, go with your heart. If it's out there in LA and that's what you really want, then you'll regret not taking the position. But if it's here, with the shop, then once it's sold… it isn't going to come back again." He said no more and just let his words linger in the air. It would be stupid for him to ask Vin to stay. He had no right, even if he desperately wanted him to remain in town so that they could see if things between them were possible.

"I know. There are a lot of things that will change if I return to LA." Vin sighed. "Hey, is that your phone?" he asked.

Casey sensed the vibration of an incoming call and pulled his phone out of his pocket. "Hey, Red," he said.

"We got 'em." He sounded thrilled. "There were three men at the field, and we got all three of them. They aren't the guys in charge, but I don't think it's going to take very much to get one of them to talk. These guys were in it for the money, and a few years in prison for growing with intent to distribute is going to loosen their tongues fast."

Casey was happy that the raid had been successful, but he wished he could have been there. "That's great."

"By the way, I talked to the chief. He knows you had nothing to do with the plants at your house, so he's expediting the investigation and wants to see the completed report soon. Hopefully you'll be back before the real fun starts."

"That would be good." He wanted to look these people in the eyes and find out what the hell they were up to. So far, he and Vin had both been directly impacted, and this shit needed to stop. "Thanks for letting me know."

"Don't worry. The chief wants you in the loop and will bring you back in as soon as he can." Red ended the call, and Casey put his phone in his pocket, then told Vin the news.

"So there were others involved. It's a good thing the state police kept looking. And with luck, one of the guys they caught will spill the real story." Vin paused, then shook his head. "Something's been bothering me. I keep wondering why Alicia and Renaldo were nosing around the greenhouse. If you wanted to talk to someone and they weren't home, wouldn't you either wait or come back? A normal person wouldn't wander around the property, taking in the sights."

Casey agreed. "Maybe when we're done here, we should take another look. You can show me where they were and exactly what they were doing. Maybe that will give us a clue as to why folks are so interested in the place. The car led us nowhere, so maybe that isn't why the place is so interesting."

"Okay. And while you're here, maybe you could help me open a box that my mother had."

Casey paused to think. "Why would you think I could do that?"

Vin shrugged. "I don't know. Mad police skills? Don't you guys have to know the same kinds of things that criminals do in order to stay ahead of them?" He was so clearly teasing. "I guess I figured you could pick a lock. But if not, I suppose I could google it."

Casey rolled his eyes. "Okay, I can try." Their conversation fell off as they approached the wooded area, and Brianna took his hand. She stayed close until they emerged in the sunlight again. Then she took off toward the play area at near full speed, waving as the laughter of the other kids drew her in like a moth to a flame. The rest of their party continued forward and found a picnic table in the shade near the play area.

Casey set down the cooler and offered drinks. The day was warm and the sun strong, so everyone was thirsty.

"How is Fred?" Mack asked Casey's mother, and then the two of them brought each other up to date on mutual friends. Casey sipped his water, watching Brianna as she played, relaxed and content. He only hoped the feeling lasted a while.

"DO WE have to go?" Brianna asked after she'd fed the ducks and played for an hour. Casey's mother had excused herself to join her garden club, so it was just the men and Brianna.

"Yes, honey. We've been here for almost two hours, and it's time we got some lunch. Why don't you go over and ask Grandma if she wants to come with us?" Casey smiled as she ran across the park. She ran back a few minutes later and said that Grandma needed fifteen more minutes. Finally she ran back to the play area. Casey sat back down with a sigh, tired simply from watching her.

"She has you wrapped around her little finger," Mack told him. "Not that that's a bad thing. She's an amazing young person. I have to give her credit—she knows what she wants and she figures out a way to get it, especially when it comes to looking after you. As I remember, she's a lot like her father."

Casey laughed. "I used to be like that."

"Then you grew up," Mack said.

"Yeah. Growing up can really mess with your dreams. When we're children, everything seems possible. And then life steps in." He watched as Brianna played. "I want all of her dreams to come true."

"That's what every parent wants for their child," Mack told him. A few minutes later, Casey's mother joined them, and Casey called Brianna.

"How about some lunch?" Vin asked. "We could walk downtown and go to the Whiskey Rebellion. Their food is good, and the onion rings are amazing. It's just a few blocks from here."

"Then let's go," Mack said. He and Casey's mother settled into a conversation together while Casey and Vin each took one of Brianna's hands, lifting her over the cracks in the sidewalk.

At the restaurant, they were escorted to a table in the dining area. They were just sitting down when—

"Casey, Clair," Alicia said as she approached the table.

Casey turned to see Renaldo sitting at a table in the corner just a few booths away, watching all of them while he talked on the phone. The restaurant grew quiet. Casey wondered if Renaldo had been following them. It would explain why he and Alicia seemed to know where he was so often. "Hi, sweetheart," Alicia said to Brianna.

"Hi, Mommy. We're here for some lunch," Brianna said and pulled her chair in closer.

"It looks like you have the whole family with you," she said, turning to Vin and Mack. "A new little family to replace what you had. Isn't that nice?"

God, the venom in her voice would drop a small animal at ten paces.

"You have your family in Costa Rica; I have mine here. It's that simple." Casey smiled and turned away. "Brianna, what do you think you'd like to eat?" He knew ignoring Alicia was the best way to get under her skin, and right now he just wanted her to leave.

Still, his back filled with tension he did his best to hide. Just having Alicia around made him paranoid, wondering what she wanted and what she was willing to do to get it. Why couldn't she just go away? He'd managed criminals with more ease than he was handling his ex-wife. Casey placed his hand flat on the table to keep it from shaking, and was about to tell Alicia where to go when the most amazing thing happened.

Vin placed his hand on his knee under the table, creating a slight pressure and warmth through his pant leg. Suddenly Casey's anxiety melted away. He wasn't alone. "I think this is going to be a wonderful lunch," Vin said. "Now, if you'll excuse us," Vin said to Alicia, "Brianna is hungry."

Just like that, Alicia had been dismissed. Mack and Casey's mother continued the conversation they'd been having about the judge who used to own the house across the street, another mutual friend. "Have you chosen what you'd like?" Vin asked Brianna, and they reviewed the menu.

Alicia looked like she'd swallowed her tongue, obviously astounded that Vin had gotten the better of her. When she didn't move, Casey added casually, "Renaldo is waiting for you." He didn't need to look to see the "if looks could kill" poison in her eyes.

"I hope you have a good trip home. Be safe." He chanced a look in her direction just in time to see her scrambling for something to say, so he beat her to it. "I really hope you decide to try to have more of a relationship with Brianna in the future. If I were you, I wouldn't let another two years go by. Maybe send her a card now and then, as well as presents for her birthday and Christmas. And, of course, the next time you're in the area, please let us know."

"How dare you?" she whispered. "I'm her mother, and I…."

Casey turned around. "Then start acting like it. You can't make up for two years of absence by barging in and making demands. Our daughter deserves better than that. And now if you'll excuse us…." He had loved her once, but that was long gone now. Still, as much as he wanted to, Casey didn't hate her. He couldn't.

Alicia turned and headed back toward where Renaldo was sitting. With a sigh, Casey put his napkin on the table and stood. "Alicia," he said quietly and as calmly as he could, slowly approaching her. "I hope you find someone who makes you happy. You deserve that." He was sad that it hadn't been him.

Casey had honestly expected a moment of understanding or maybe a nod of acknowledgment, but all he received was a frigid stare before she turned away. Maybe he had no right to expect anything else. Alicia had been hurt, and he knew he was partly to blame for not seeing who she was and being honest about himself, but unfortunately, much of her pain now was of her own making.

Alicia slid into the booth with Renaldo as he spoke rapidly to someone on the phone. "But *have* you seen Pederman lately…?" he asked a little urgently. Then, after lifting his gaze to Casey for just a second, he turned his attention back to his call, speaking much lower this time… and largely ignoring Alicia, which seemed to irk her even more.

Casey returned to the table and sat down.

"You okay?" Vin asked half under his breath.

Casey forced a smile and then, slowly, it felt more genuine. "Yes." He rubbed his hands together. "What are we going to order to go with our onion rings?" It was time he started living again—really living—and that meant looking forward instead of back. Casey only wished he knew what kind of picture was forming in that direction. But only time would fill in the broad outlines with any sort of detail.

"Yay," Brianna said, and Casey placed an order with their server. He'd worked up quite an appetite.

"IS GRANDMA gonna walk home with us?" Brianna asked as they left the restaurant.

"No, sweetheart," she said, giving Brianna a hug. "But I'll see you soon, and we have dance class next week." Then she stood and kissed Casey's cheek. "I like Vin," she whispered.

Casey paused as he pulled back. "That must taste like chalk about now."

His mother rolled her eyes. "And don't think I don't know where he kept his hand through much of lunch. He calmed you down when you were talking to

Alicia, I know that." She patted his shoulder. "Maybe he is good for you. But if he hurts you, I'll still rip his nuts off." His mother added the last part under her breath, sending him into a coughing fit. By the time he caught his breath, she was too far away for him to respond. Still, the show of support was appreciated.

Once she'd left them, he, Vin, Mack, and Brianna crossed the street and walked home. After a lunch like that, they needed it. Casey's shepherd's pie was wonderful, and Vin had given him a taste of his chicken pot pie, which was also good. Thankfully, Brianna hadn't filled up on onion rings and had eaten some of her chicken.

The walk did them all good, and once they got back to the house, Mack went inside to rest, while Brianna played with her doll under one of the shade trees in the yard. "Promise me you'll stay here. Vin and I need to take a look at the greenhouse. We'll be right over there." He pointed.

"Yes, Daddy," she answered as if she was the parent.

Mack came out the back door. "I'll watch her," he said, sitting in the shade. Satisfied that Brianna would be okay, Casey and Vin walked across the little-traveled back street to the shop.

"Where exactly did you see them?" Casey asked.

Vin led him around to the back of the greenhouse. "They were coming around this corner when I came out of the house. They seemed to be looking at the ground, but I can't be sure. They were certainly interested in the outside of the building."

Casey scratched his head. "I don't understand what they could have been looking for. There's nothing out here but overgrown weeds and grass." Along with a few bits of scrub that were beginning to take root near the structure. "Is that where the pane of glass was removed for access?" Casey asked, and Vin nodded.

"I put it back into place."

Casey knelt down, examining the area. "It's trampled down, so they were using this for a period of time. Not that we didn't already know that." He stood, looking around. "When you had your visitors that first night, did you see which way they went? I doubt they parked on the street or right here behind the building. They'd need to find a place where they wouldn't raise suspicion." The grasses had grown up behind the building, so there wasn't much of a path left.

"Personally, I'd park over there." Vin headed toward what might have been an alley at the end of the road, but it ended in a driveway. He walked over to it. "Look. Someone has been parking here." He knelt down, pointing but not touching. "And from the looks of it, they've been sampling their own products."

Casey nodded and left the evidence in place. It was way down at the base of the grass and unlikely to have been seen. It seemed Vin had gotten lucky. They searched the grass before moving into the scrub brush at the edge of the alley. Casey slowly walked back toward the greenhouse, looking from side to side, remembering that it had been dark when the perps were here, and if they'd dropped anything, they might not have been able to find it again. He paused, bending deeper into the brush, then stood up and pulled out his phone to take a picture of what looked to be a black notebook in the underbrush.

"Red, I need you to come to the greenhouse at Vin's. I—" He didn't have a chance to finish his thought.

A scream split the air and then was cut off. Casey knew that tone and raced around the side of the greenhouse, taking off across the yard. Renaldo had Brianna in his arms, his hand over her mouth, and was carrying her toward the car parked outside Vin's house. It took Casey a second before he realized that he still had his phone.

"Casey," Red was shouting.

"Renaldo is trying to kidnap Brianna." He didn't stop and didn't remember dropping the phone. All he knew was that he took off full tilt toward the car, approaching the road as Renaldo slammed the rear passenger door and jumped into the driver's side, then took off. Casey reached the street just in time to see the taillights brighten and then round the corner.

"Casey!" Vin said as he caught up, pressing his phone into his hands. Sirens sounded and grew closer, tires squealing as Red skidded to a stop. Casey pulled open the door and jumped in, barely realizing that Vin got in the back.

"Turn left on Bedford. It's a gray Mercedes. The same one Carter researched." Red called it in and took off like a bat out of hell, whipping the car around and back toward the main road as the Mercedes passed right in front of them, most likely making for the highway.

Renaldo turned south on I-81, and Red followed right behind him.

"Get on to the state police," Red instructed. "Tell them what's happened and where we're heading.

Our jurisdiction ends, and we can stay on their tail, but support is going to be needed." Red kept his siren and lights going while Casey fumbled to make the call. His hands shook so badly, and all he could think about was Brianna in that car, scared to death.

"We're going to find her," Vin said from the back seat. They couldn't touch because of the security barricade, but Casey wished to hell they could. Casey made the call and got confirmation that the state police would close the highway about five miles ahead.

"They're passing mile 45. Gray Mercedes," he said, then repeated the license plate. "We're behind him, but he's weaving in and out of traffic. It's only a matter of time before he loses control. His movements are too erratic."

"It's going to be okay," Vin said again as Red went even faster, pushing the car to its limits. Fortunately traffic ahead was clearing, and as they approached Exit 43, the Mercedes fishtailed and slowed, allowing them to get closer.

"They're going to take the exit," Casey said, but the driver veered away and continued on. Red did the same. "We have to be approaching the closure."

Taillights appeared ahead, and vehicles started to slow as they saw police vehicles stretched out across the lanes. There was nowhere for the Mercedes to go, and Casey breathed a sigh for about two seconds—until the car turned onto the grass median and fishtailed before reaching the other lane. Now the car was heading back the way they'd come.

Red did the same, flying fast enough they might have left the ground. Vin groaned from the back seat.

"You okay back there?" Red called without looking away.

"I'm fine. Just go!" Vin said between clenched teeth. "Get Brianna back."

Casey made more calls and was informed that the entire freeway had been closed. All exits were now blocked for the next ten miles, and traffic was coming to a complete standstill all the way to Mechanicsburg. Taillights once again appeared, and Renaldo tried again to cross the median, only this time he misjudged its steepness.

Casey paled and held his breath as the Mercedes took the embankment at the wrong angle, heading down. At first he thought the car was going to roll, but then it corrected just enough that it reached the bottom of the embankment and started upward, but without enough purchase for the wheels to grab and move forward. There was a highway sign directly in its path.

Casey's eyes closed and he prayed as the Mercedes hit it, the high-pitched crash of metal and breaking glass hitting him right in the heart.

Red slowed the car, and Casey was out of it as soon as it stopped, with Red right behind him. The driver's door of the Mercedes opened slowly, and Renaldo stumbled out. Red tackled him to the ground and cuffed and arrested him on the spot. Casey went to the driver's door, unlocked the car, then he pulled open the door to the back seat. Alicia lay across the seat, apparently stunned. She was breathing, but Casey barely noticed. Brianna lay on top of her.

"Sweetheart, it's me. Are you okay?" Brianna groaned and moved slightly. "Brianna. Can you hear me?"

"Daddy?" she asked, and the elephant that had been sitting on his chest the entire time finally got off.

"What hurts? Can you breathe okay?" He looked her over, afraid to move her in case she was badly injured.

"Get her out!" Red yelled. "I smell gas."

Without thinking twice, he carefully lifted Brianna into his arms and out of the car and carried her back toward Red's patrol car. It was then he saw Vin staring at him from out the back window. Casey gently set Brianna down and unlocked the doors. Vin climbed out and knelt next to Brianna. "What hurts?"

"My arm," Brianna whimpered.

"Okay. Does it hurt to breathe?" Vin asked, and Brianna shook her head. "Can you feel me touching your legs?"

"Yes, Mr. Vin." She tried to smile, but it faded quickly.

"Does your back or head hurt?" Vin asked, and Brianna said no. "Can you sit here with me while your daddy helps Mr. Red?" Vin asked, and he sat down next to her and let her lean on him. "Go. Take care of business."

Casey hurried back to the car and helped Red get Alicia out and away just as the back of the car burst into flame. It didn't explode the way cars did in the movies, but the ground and the trunk were quickly engulfed. Casey got everyone a safe distance away as more vehicles arrived.

The fire department doused the flames while ambulances pulled up. Alicia was conscious, but barely. She really seemed out of it. Some of his fellow officers arrived and took custody of Renaldo. Alicia was loaded into an ambulance after officially being taken into custody.

Brianna was up and walking, refusing to go anywhere near the ambulance, half clinging to Casey while favoring her injured arm. It wasn't until he told her that he'd go with her that Brianna allowed herself to be put in the ambulance. Casey rode along, holding her good hand as they covered the short distance to the hospital.

"Is Mommy hurt bad?" Brianna asked.

"I don't know," Casey answered, barely managing to control his anger. "What did she do?"

Brianna sniffed, and Casey gently stroked her hair. "That man pushed Mr. Mack, then grabbed me and put his hand over my mouth. I screamed like you told me to, and then he put me in the back with Mommy." More sniffles followed.

"You're a very brave girl." He hated that his daughter was hurting and willed the ambulance to get to the hospital quickly so they could make her feel better.

"Mommy said that we were going to where she lived because you didn't want me anymore. She said that you said that she could have me and that we were going to her house in Costa Rica."

Casey leaned closer. "I will always want you—I promise you that. Your mother was lying to you. I would never let anyone take you from me, ever." He squeezed her hand, wiping the tears from her cheeks.

"You're my best girl, and I'll always love you. Nothing will ever change that."

Brianna sniffed. "Even if you love Mr. Vin?" Sometimes she saw way more than Casey ever gave her credit for.

"Yes. Even if I love Mr. Vin. That doesn't mean I will ever stop loving you." He rested his cheek on her head, willing the tears that threatened back inside. "You'll always be my special girl." What the hell had Alicia been thinking? He couldn't help wondering how badly she was hurt. Whatever it was, he hoped it was painful… very painful.

The ambulance eventually pulled to a stop in front of the hospital. The EMTs got Brianna out and brought her inside, with Casey right beside her, holding her good hand. "You're being so brave."

"My arm hurts," Brianna whined as Vin hurried up to them.

"Red brought me in. Dad is okay, just a little shaken up, but he'll be okay now that he knows she's back with you," he said gently. "How are you, sweetheart?" he asked Brianna. "It's going to be okay. Once you're all patched up, why don't we stop off and get you a big bowl of ice cream? You deserve it after this." He flashed a smile and got one in return.

A nurse came up to Casey. "Are you her father?" When he nodded, she asked, "And him?"

"He's a close family friend. And he'll be coming with us." He was ready if she challenged him, but the nurse simply guided Brianna back into an examination room, where she took her pulse, temperature, and blood pressure.

"Am I gonna have a shot?" Brianna asked.

"Maybe, honey," Casey said. "But don't worry. I'll hold your hand the entire time. And Mr. Vin will be here too. Just close your eyes and maybe take a nap. Okay, honey?" He continued holding her hand as she closed her eyes. Casey looked over her to where Vin sat.

"She's going to be fine," Vin said.

Casey nodded. "I don't know if I will be. I swear I aged a decade in the last few hours." The thought of anything happening to Brianna made him cold once again.

"Red said that he's taking care of things back at the station but that he'll be in later to talk to both of you. He wants to make sure everything is perfectly clear in the reports. He doesn't want there to be any chance of Renaldo getting out."

Vin came around and stood next to him, silently offering support. Casey put an arm around his waist and rested his head against his side. His anxiety seemed to settle almost instantly.

If he closed his eyes, Casey could almost see the three of them as a family… as long as he didn't think out too far. His little vision of perfection was fragile, and he knew it. Still, for the time being, he held on to it as they waited for the doctor to come in and tell them the plan.

TWO HOURS later, her arm encased in a pink cast, Brianna asked, "Can we go home now? I'm hungry, and Mr. Vin promised ice cream." She had a mind like a steel trap when it came to ice cream.

"I know. We all are," Casey said, thankful that the break wasn't too bad. Brianna's arm would have to be in the cast for the next month. He'd explained that she wasn't going to be able to go swimming while she had it on and that she was going to have to take it easy. She hadn't been happy about that.

Casey's parents had been furious when they'd heard the news. He'd stepped out of the room to call them once he knew they were dealing with a simple fracture. "I'll kill that woman" had been his mother's reaction.

"She's in surgery right now, and the universe may give you your wish." Alicia had apparently shielded Brianna from the majority of the force of the impact. She had hit her head, and as time passed, pressure had built around her brain. Surgeons were working to relieve it, but they weren't sure how severe the injuries were, given how quickly she'd deteriorated. In any case, Casey silently wished her the best. "The important thing is that Brianna is okay," he reminded her. Casey had already told himself that nearly a hundred times.

Casey signed all the forms, and Red pulled his SUV up in front of the hospital. Casey climbed in the back with Brianna and buckled her in, then sat next to her while Vin climbed in the passenger seat.

"Take them to my dad's, please," Vin said. "There's something we need you to see while we're there."

Casey had completely forgotten about the small black notebook they'd seen earlier.

"Dad is already making dinner, and this one is going to need to rest once she's filled up on ice cream."

"Thank you." The thought of trying to do anything right now was more than he could bear.

Red pulled out, and they were quiet for most of the ride home.

"Do you want to join us?" Casey heard Vin ask Red as he pulled Brianna out of the back seat of the SUV. He carried Brianna inside and put her on the sofa. Mack sat down next to her.

"I need to go with Mr. Red for a few minutes. Mr. Mack will stay here with you. I'm not going to be gone for very long. Okay?" Casey asked. Mack already had cartoons on, and Brianna seemed comfortable.

Casey then led Vin and Red out toward the greenhouse. Red passed him some gloves, and he pulled them on, found the spot, and retrieved the book. He paged through it and grinned.

"What is it?" Vin asked.

"The smoking gun. It seems one of the customers—a guy named Nathan—kept notes on what he bought and what he sold. It looks like this also contains a list of suppliers, customers, amounts, dates… you name it. This guy sure did his homework." Casey shook his head in wonder. "No wonder Renaldo and Alicia were so anxious to find it. The book has been there long enough that some of the pages are wet from the rain we had a week ago." He slowly paged through it. "I'd say that everyone involved in this little venture was scared enough to shit bricks." He paused, checking that he was seeing what he thought, and showed the page to Red and Vin. "It looks like we've found all the proof we need to put Renaldo away for a while."

"What about Alicia?" Vin asked. "Do you think she knew what he was doing?"

"When Casey called me, I was doing a little investigating of my own. As we know, Renaldo's and Alicia's families are really close. And after some digging, I've been in contact with a family member who has no love for Alicia—one who is quite happy to talk to us. According to my source, Alicia is claiming that because Renaldo had business here, he told her that he could help her get access to her daughter. And apparently she leapt at the chance."

Red took the book and looked through it with a smile. "Not only does this list Renaldo as his supplier, but Nathan put his own name in here and listed everyone he thought was involved with the operation. Apparently he wanted to be able to get revenge should anyone turn on him. Either this guy was brilliant or dumb as a stump."

Casey chuckled. "Let's go with brilliant. At least from our perspective." He sighed, the adrenaline from the day's excitement wearing off. "Do you think we have this guy in custody already?"

"I don't know. But I bet the guys we do have will be falling over each other to tell us what we want to know, trying to cut a deal." Red slipped the book into an evidence bag and tagged it. "I need to get this over to the station and talk to the chief. I'm willing to bet that this little gem is going to create a lot of work for the department in the next few days. Everyone is going to want to be able to see how many cases this helps them close." He jogged back toward the car, and Vin took Casey's hand.

"Come on. There's a little girl who needs her daddy right now, and I need to help Dad with dinner. Then, once I get you home and Brianna is tucked in bed asleep, maybe I can put her daddy to bed and see how much of this excitement I can help him forget. At least for a few hours." Vin kissed him, and Casey held him tight, needing Vin to help him forget the worst day of his life.

BRIANNA WAS wired by the time Casey got her home. Vin gave them a ride and helped them get settled inside. The hospital had given Casey some pain medication for Brianna, and once she started complaining about her arm hurting, he got her ready for bed and gave her a painkiller and a glass of water before settling her under the covers. He read her a story, and thankfully Brianna was out before he got halfway through.

Or at least he thought she was. "Daddy, my arm still hurts. It might feel better if I had a dog to cuddle with."

"It will feel better soon, I promise."

"But Daddy…."

"I'll think about it, okay? For now, though, just go to sleep. Your arm will feel better in the morning. I promise."

Brianna smiled as she settled under the covers, as if she had already won. Casey knew he wasn't going to be able to hold out much longer. In fact, he was no longer sure why he was holding out at all. He looked again at his little girl. She'd been so brave, and during the abduction, she'd done exactly what he'd always told her to do—scream. Would it really be so bad to give her something she wanted so badly?

"Listen, if we do get a dog, we have to get one from a rescue, and your grandma is going to have to agree too, because she watches you during the day. And the puppy will have to go to her house too." Getting that agreement was going to be a lot easier said than done.

"Okay, Daddy. Thank you!" Then she rolled over, her cast resting on a pillow, and in minutes, she was asleep.

Casey was exhausted when he joined Vin downstairs. "Brianna hit me up for a puppy again, and in a moment of weakness, I caved. I did tell her that Mom would have to agree too, because the dog would need to be at her place sometimes." He sat down next to Vin. "Mitchell Brannigan is a local vet, and he runs a dog rescue. Maybe we should go out there and see if he has one that will be suitable. That's where Red and Terry got their dog."

Vin leaned against him. "Why not just take her down there tomorrow and let her pick out a dog herself?"

"My mother…."

"Will come around easily. One look into a cute puppy face and your mother will fall right into line. Besides, I think she'll do just about anything to make up for taking Alicia's side after what she and Renaldo pulled." Vin smiled up at him. "Use it to your full advantage. Remember that sometimes a little guilt can be a good thing."

Casey laughed, and it felt so good. "You know Brianna will be over the moon."

"Then let's see what they have. I don't think the problem is going to be finding a dog. It'll be that she wants all of them." Vin paused. "Maybe Dad should come with us. A dog would be great company for him."

Casey nodded. "I guess it's a go, then. Contact Mitchell in the morning and let him know we're coming. I can't think of a more wonderful shopping trip. And it will make Brianna really happy." The way he grinned was infectious.

"Can't you just imagine the way her eyes will light up? I bet it will take her hours to pick one out." Vin seemed almost excited as Brianna was sure to be.

Casey could easily see that. "I just want her to be able to forget all about what happened today. But I know it's not that simple. I'll have to get her some help so she can process it." There was no way he wanted Brianna to go through this on her own. He had no idea what sort of notions Brianna was going to develop, but he wasn't going to have his daughter thinking that she was to blame for anything. Already he was wondering if he should have done something differently, something that would have stopped the events of the day from occurring.

"Just stop it," Vin said, leaning closer. "I know you're a cop and all, but there's no way you could have known that your ex-wife was going to pull something like this. How could you possibly have had any idea?" Casey stared at Vin, wondering if he could read his mind. "Please. I've known you forever, and I know how you're feeling right now. But it's bullshit. My dad was with her. You didn't leave Brianna alone, and they must have swept in fast. If anything, you being so close saved her. They weren't going to get away, not with a police officer on their tail from the very beginning."

"But…." Casey's throat ached, and he clamped his eyes closed. "What sort of father does it make me that I couldn't stop them?"

"The father who jumped into action and had all of us minutes behind them. You and Red would have trailed them down the freeway forever until you got her back. I have no doubt of that." Vin tugged him close. "Stop beating yourself up. Brianna is right upstairs. Alicia is in the hospital, and regardless of whether she recovers or not, she's not getting near Brianna anytime soon. Renaldo is behind bars, and that's where he's going to stay. So now the rest is up to you."

Vin could say that, but it wasn't true. Casey knew that the rest—at least the rest of what he wanted—was up to Vin. Because while Brianna was asleep in her bed and hopefully dreaming of happier things than car chases and kidnappers, Casey couldn't seem to get the image of the three of them as a family out of his mind. What he wanted was very clear, but actually managing to make it happen was a completely different issue.

Maybe in that longing for a life that held everything he'd ever wanted, he could understand, just a little, why Alicia would do something as stupid as try to abduct Brianna. Not that he would ever do anything that destructive or hurtful, but he could understand the longing behind it. Especially since the thought of Vin leaving at the end of the week tore his heart apart.

CHAPTER 9

VIN WANTED to help, but he didn't know what to do. Casey seemed lost in his thoughts, and while Vin didn't want to disturb him, he didn't want Casey to wallow in them either. He shuffled closer and lightly stroked along his whisker-rough jaw with just the tips of his fingers. "Casey," he said gently, and he could feel his attention snap back to him. "You can't let this pull you in."

"I'm doing my best." Casey stood and began pacing the room. "It's different for you. You like Brianna, I know you do, but it's different when you're a parent. The thought of anything happening to her makes my stomach clench and my heart scream in agony."

"I know that," he said. "And I know I'm not a parent. But she's upstairs safe in her bed, and that's because of you." He stood as well, cupping Casey's head in his hands. "So let's get this straight right now. You did everything you could… and it worked. She's safe. You're the best dad I've ever met. So let's skip the recriminations. There shouldn't be any. At least, not on your part." Alicia, though, was another matter. What sort of mother would put her child through that?

"I know you're right. But that isn't the problem," Casey said, and Vin understood—it was Casey's marriage to an unstable woman that had created the whole mess. But something good came out of it too. So he started turning out the lights and took Casey by the hand, then led him up the stairs to Brianna's door.

She was sound asleep under her pink blanket, a stuffed doll tucked up under her chin, the arm in a cast on a pillow of its own. "See, there she is," Vin said. "Right where she should be. In her own bed, in the house with you. The doors are locked, and if you want me to, I'll stay downstairs and guard the place all night long so both of you can sleep. No one will come anywhere near either one of you." Dammit, he needed them to be safe and protected.

Vin had never seen himself as the protective type. He was a florist, a rather artsy kind of guy who designed arrangements and showpieces. But when it came to these two, he'd sit up all night watching old movies and drinking coffee so they could sleep undisturbed. Hell, he'd take on anyone who tried to hurt either of them with his bare hands if he had to.

"There's no need for that," Casey said, still watching Brianna sleep. Then he stepped back from her door and took a single step toward his own room. "But I don't think I can handle being alone right now."

Vin followed him. "You aren't alone. No matter where I am, you aren't going to be alone." He followed Casey into the room and closed the door.

At this point, Vin had no intention of doing anything more active tonight than cleaning up, getting undressed, and climbing under the covers with Casey. It was impossible for him to understand the worry and anxiety that Casey felt, but he had to do something to help him. So he got undressed, then slid under the covers and waited for Casey.

He stayed awake for a long time, but eventually his eyes grew heavy. He figured Casey was in with Brianna, reassuring himself that she was truly going to be okay. Vin propped himself up on the pillow, listening for the soft creak of the floorboards.

It came five minutes later, and then the door opened. Casey stepped inside and closed the door, a sense of calm in his features. "She's sound asleep, but I had to look in on her one more time just to make sure she was fine." Casey came around the bed, gliding slowly, and Vin followed him with his gaze until Casey slipped under the covers.

Vin turned out the lights and rolled over, slipped his hands over Casey's belly, and pulled him closer. He closed his eyes and expected to settle in. But Casey slowly rolled him back, and Casey's lips found his. The need in that kiss was nearly overwhelming. Casey shook, and Vin held on, giving as good as he received.

"Vin…."

"I know," Vin whispered. Casey didn't need to say the words. He easily communicated what he desperately wanted, and Vin stroked his cheek for a few seconds. Then he wound his hands down Casey's back, holding him close.

Vin rolled them on the bed, pulled the last of Casey's clothes off, then pushed away the bedding until he lay bare before him. "Vin… I…." Nodding in acknowledgment of what Casey couldn't say, Vin slid his lips around the head of Casey's cock, then slowly deeper, taking more of him as Casey's desperation and movements became faster, more demanding.

Vin relaxed, letting Casey take what he needed, allowing him to work through his demons. But like so many things in life, energy and desire are contagious, and Vin was soon carried away by Casey. He let Casey guide him and gave him everything he needed until neither of them could hold back any longer. Only when they'd both come in a climax that made the earth move did Vin back away and lie next to Casey, holding him while a wave of pure, raw emotion crashed over him. Vin was grateful the lights were out—they'd hide Casey's tears that flowed now that he'd finally let go. But Vin was very much aware of the trails of dampness that slid down his own cheeks.

VIN WOKE the following morning to find Casey curled against him, holding him, and every time he moved, Casey's arm tightened slightly, pulling him closer. He was pretty sure that Casey was still asleep and that the reaction was visceral and deep. Even in his sleep, which had been fitful and jerky all night, Casey had kept him close. Vin tried to go back to sleep, but without much luck.

There was a knock, and then the door opened. Brianna came in to stand by the bed. "I'm hungry and my arm hurts," she said softly.

"Your daddy is still asleep," Vin said, very aware that under the covers, they were both naked. "Can you play with your dolls for a few minutes and I'll get up and make you some breakfast? Do you think that will make your arm feel better?"

Brianna nodded and left the room. Vin hurried to get dressed and then took Brianna downstairs. She was still in her Barbie nightgown, but that was okay. Vin knew that Brianna had been prescribed something for pain, but he felt that Casey should be the one to give her the medication. So Vin got her settled on the sofa under a blanket and put some cartoons on for her to watch while he got breakfast together. He blinked when he saw the time. It was after nine. Then again, after yesterday, Casey could use all the rest he could get. Vin made some scrambled eggs and toast, then brought a small plate in for Brianna.

"What about Daddy?" she asked after taking a few bites.

"He's still asleep," Vin answered. "He can have some when he gets up." He sat at the foot of the sofa and ate his own eggs. Brianna ate most of what he'd given her and then settled back under the blanket. She didn't fuss or cry for Casey, and Vin suddenly realized just how much he'd been accepted by this little family—and how special that was. He fit in here, and the thought of leaving left him cold.

This was what he'd been looking for his entire life—a place he truly belonged. And here it was, right back with the man he'd known since he was a kid. The thought of leaving was painful, yet the idea of staying scared him to death. Leaving meant jetting across the country and saying goodbye to these two people who had stolen his heart. But what he'd wanted for so long—or thought he wanted—was waiting for him in California. He'd have partial ownership of the shop and a shot at a future he could build for himself.

Staying here for Casey and Brianna… it terrified him. He wanted Casey so badly it hurt, but he couldn't help worrying about what he'd do if things didn't work out. He and Casey had reconnected less than a week ago, and the almost frantic pace of the reawakening of his feelings left him delighted and frightened. He could so easily get used to having these two people in his life. Vin didn't know what he was going to do. There was no easy answer.

"Sweetheart," Casey said as he entered the room, his hair still disheveled and his eyes half-lidded. "How's your arm?"

"It hurts, but not as much as yesterday," she answered as Casey hugged her carefully.

"I can give you a pill, but it will make you sleepy." Which probably wasn't a bad thing. Rest was what she needed, and Vin needed a chance to think. But he wasn't going to be that lucky. "Why don't you go upstairs and get dressed? Mr. Vin and

I are going to take you to find yourself a dog." He yawned and still seemed tired, especially around the eyes, but Brianna was suddenly filled with energy.

"Daddy!" she squealed and hurried over to hug him before racing up the stairs, her pain forgotten. Vin wished his life was that simple.

"Do you want something to eat?" Vin asked Casey, who shook his head.

"I just want to be able to stop worrying. I actually checked out front before I came down to make sure that Mercedes wasn't out there. And when I got up and Brianna wasn't in her room, this panic grabbed my stomach until I realized she was downstairs with you." He closed his eyes as Vin pulled him into his arms.

"I don't know what you're going through, but I was scared to death too. The thought of anything happening to her…." Vin swallowed hard. "Or of you going through that kind of pain…." He closed his eyes and held Casey tighter. "But she's okay and excited about looking at dogs. Just like any normal kid would be."

"I know. That's part of what scares me. She seems to be taking this in stride, and I don't understand it. Why isn't she more upset, or…?"

Vin didn't have the answer. "Maybe when we get back, you should sit down with her and ask her how she feels. Maybe there's something we don't know. Let her give voice to what she thinks. It might help both of you."

Casey closed his arms around him. "Of course." His grip tightened. "What would I do without you?"

Vin stroked up Casey's back, cupping his head in his hands and wishing to hell he had an answer for that. He needed to make up his mind. Because Casey deserved to know what was going to happen so he could be prepared.

"DADDY, THERE are so many!" Brianna said happily as they walked through the shelter. Dog after dog wagged its tail, a few barking, while others seemed to hide.

"I know," Casey said while Vin held a small terrier named Oscar.

The dog settled right into Vin's arms and looked up at him adoringly. The thought of letting him go was too much, so Vin called his father to ask if he wanted a dog. After sending pictures and messages, it seemed his father was on his way too, and before long, the little guy had won over his heart as well. Vin had already started the paperwork for his father, and by the time all the details had been taken care of, Vin's stoic father had turned into a bowl of dog-loving mush.

"You need to decide which dog you like best," Casey told Brianna as Mitchell, the veterinarian and operator of the rescue, stood nearby, smiling broadly.

"It's a hard decision, isn't it?" Mitchell asked Brianna. "Do you want a big dog, or a smaller one? It's important not only to love your dog but to be able to care for it properly. That means taking the dog for walks, feeding it, and caring for it."

Brianna nodded as though she were taking in every word. "So, since I'm little, I should get a small dog. That way I can walk him." She smiled and turned toward a Maltese-poodle mix that was about two years old. He had a scar above one eye but all the energy in the world. Mitchell got him out of the cage, and Brianna took him gently, and Vin saw her fall in love—just like that. Vin took Casey's hand and squeezed it.

"Is that the one you want?"

Brianna nodded.

"His name is Winston," Mitchell said. "You could change it, but he already knows that name, so it's easier if it stays the same."

"I like Winston," Brianna pronounced.

Casey nodded, then set to work filling out forms while Mitchell got a leash and showed her how to walk the dog out in the yard.

"This was the perfect idea," Casey said as he snapped pictures of Brianna and Winston, probably to send to his mother. Mitchell brought both Casey and his dad up to date on the care of the dogs, including information on their schedule for shots and other treatments.

By the time they were ready to go, both Vin's dad and Brianna were beaming. His dad put Oscar's carrier in his car and was about to leave when his phone rang. He sat on the edge of the back seat with the door open and talked on the phone while Vin helped Casey load the supplies for Winston into the back of the car.

"What is it, Dad?" Vin asked as his father hung up.

"I got an offer on the shop," he said.

Vin sighed. "That's good. Are they going to operate it as a florist?"

His dad shrugged. "It doesn't really matter. Once it's sold, that's it." He put his phone away and got to his feet, closed the back door, and got behind the wheel. "I'll see you at home. The realtor will bring over the offer at five, and I'm hoping you can be there to take a look at it." He started the engine and pulled out. Vin had expected his father to be more excited, but he seemed really down.

"What was that about?" Casey asked as he joined him.

"Someone has put an offer on the shop," Vin said, blinking as he tried to think about what that meant. His father wasn't going to have to worry about the property any longer. That was a good thing, but Vin realized that part of his mother was also going to disappear. She had been the one to put her heart and soul in the place, and now it would be gone. "He wants me to be there with him when the realtor goes over the offer."

"Of course," Casey told him softly. "By all means you should go and see what the deal is. What time will she be there?"

Vin checked his phone. "This afternoon about five."

"Let me finish up here. Then we'll drop you off at your dad's place, and I can get Brianna home with her dog." He turned away, moving more stiffly than usual. Vin noticed the coolness in Casey's voice, and he didn't blame him for a second. It was obvious he was preparing himself for the inevitable. Vin was going home in a few days, and even with all the time they had spent together in the past week, the excitement, drama… everything was going to end. Vin couldn't blame Casey for wanting to put a little distance between them.

THE RIDE home was quiet. Casey drove and said very little. Brianna talked in the back, but mostly to the dog in the carrier next to her. "This doesn't change anything," Vin said.

Casey shook his head. "It changes everything," he said quietly, and Vin realized that just like his father, Casey had been hoping that the shop and greenhouse would give Vin a reason to stay. Vin had to admit that he'd been tempted. "You're leaving, and I'm going to have to figure out how to get along without you again." He took a deep breath. "I knew this was going to happen, and I went into things with my eyes open." He pulled to a stop at the light on the edge of town. "None of this is your fault, but it's difficult to know that the person you've fallen for is going to leave."

"Did you fall, Daddy? Do you need a Band-Aid? I have Dora ones at home," Brianna said from the back seat.

"No, sweetheart, I'm fine," Casey said, but his voice was rough. "I'm not going to ask you to stay because that wouldn't be fair." He took Vin's hand. "But I want you to know that I'd like you to." He made the turn in town, crossed the main street, and then drove to Vin's father's house.

"Can Winston and I get out?" Brianna asked.

"Yes. But I have to put his leash on, and you can't just let him run. It's too open, and we don't want him to run away. Okay?" Casey sounded worn out, and Vin knew some of that was because of him. Still, he got Brianna and Winston out, and she held his leash, the two of them taking off across the yard. The fact that she had one arm in a sling didn't stop her for a second.

Casey closed the door, and they moved into the shade of one of the huge old trees that lined the property. "I want you to know that I want you to stay. I know that's asking a lot. So I'm not going to ask. But I can't stay quiet and just let you go either."

"Casey, I…." Vin's heart ached.

"I know. I'd ask you to stay, but I… I don't want you to stay for me. I know it sounds stupid, but I want you to stay for you. Stay because you want to." He looked into Vin's eyes with such pleading that Vin was tempted to say yes just to get him to stop. "I know your dad wants you to stay as well."

Vin nodded, looking back toward the house, the curtains falling into place as his father moved back from the window. "I know." He took a deep breath. "But neither of you has any idea what you're asking." He swallowed hard and dug deep. "Look, I left town years ago because there was nothing for me here. I wanted more, and I've found it. I can own half the shop now, and because Sue wants to step back, I can call more of the shots. I can make that place my own. It's what I've always wanted, and…." He sighed, his chest pounding. "Things were so hard here when I was growing up. A gay kid in this little town where everyone knew everything. I was scared all the damned time. You remember what it was like?"

Casey nodded. "But it isn't like that anymore."

"I know that—in my head. But part of me is still afraid that everything is going to return to that. At the shop in LA, I can be the floral designer who makes the impossible happen. Here I'm just going to be the Robins kid who does flowers." It was hard for him to put his feelings into words.

"You're a lot more than that," Casey protested. "And I know it's probably ridiculous to expect you to just uproot your life… but this is home."

"It's not my home."

"Is LA really your home?" Casey asked, and Vin hesitated. He hated that, but it happened anyway. "Maybe that's what you need to figure out." Casey drew closer. "What feels like home?"

Vin closed his eyes, because that was an easy question. Casey and Brianna felt like home. But they weren't his, no matter what he might think or feel. The entire world couldn't change in a matter of days, and he couldn't give up his entire livelihood simply because of a visit back home…. Even his own thoughts betrayed him.

"It sounds to me like you still have things you need to figure out." Casey embraced him. "Just know that there are people here who want you to stay, and we don't want anything from you other than you." Casey held him for a while, and Vin thought about fighting it but settled into that warm embrace. It made him feel like this was where he belonged. Dammit. Why was it that everything just made this decision harder?

"I need to check on Dad and see what's going on with him and Oscar."

Casey didn't let him go, and Vin sighed, holding him in return. "I don't know what to do, Casey. That's what has me all turned around. Going back to LA is the sure bet. I have an opportunity waiting for me there that I know and understand. Here, everything is unknown. What if things don't work out between us?"

"But what if they do?" Casey asked. "What if the three of us create a family of our own?"

Dammit. Casey had played the family card. "But what if that's not what I'm meant for? Things could go just as cold between us as they've been hot all this week. I wish I was one of those people who could just chuck it all for love, jump in with both feet, and damn the torpedoes."

Casey released him and pulled back. "So do I, Vin. I wish that more than anything." He stepped away and called to Brianna, who ran over with Winston. "You and I need to get home. We have things to do."

"Is Mr. Vin going to have a sleepover again?" she asked, and Casey turned to him.

"I don't think so." He got the dog into the carrier and back in the car.

Vin stood alone, watching as Casey packed up and got ready to leave. Brianna waved, and he did the same in return, walking to the edge of the road as Casey put the car in gear and drove away. He couldn't help himself—he watched the taillights until the car turned the corner. Then he went inside to see what his dad was up to.

VIN'S FATHER sat on the sofa with Oscar standing next to him, tail wagging as his dad petted him. As soon as he saw Vin, Oscar jumped down and raced over, then ran around his legs until Vin bent down to give him some attention. "I think he's going to be a really good dog." He smiled, and Oscar bounded around for a few moments before joining his dad on the sofa once again, this time settling right down.

"Where's Casey?" His dad gently stroked Oscar's head. Maybe Vin should have suggested his dad get a dog years ago.

"He and Brianna went home," Vin answered, really not wanting to talk about how he'd screwed things up. He went to the kitchen to avoid his father.

"When is he coming back? Or are you going over there after we meet with the realtor?" he asked, and Vin purposely didn't answer. "Vin?" Now he sounded suspicious. "What's going on?"

Vin grabbed a bottle of water from the refrigerator and joined his dad in the family room. "I screwed up, okay? But I'm going back to LA in a few days and…."

His father rolled his eyes. "Sometimes you can be so damned stubborn." He got up and left the room, calling for Oscar, who followed him up the stairs.

"What?" Vin asked, and his dad paused. "Why is everyone after me all of a sudden?"

His dad came back down and lowered himself into one of the front living room chairs, which were still just where his mother had placed them. "Son, I can't tell you what to do. No one can. But dammit, you're my son, and like it or not, I know you. When someone tries to make you do something, you dig in your heels and resist with everything you have. I've seen you do it more times than I can count."

Vin couldn't argue with that. "So I'm supposed to just leave everything and…."

His dad smiled. "I know that can be frightening, but sometimes you just have to take a leap and trust that you'll land where you're meant to be."

"I'm not scared, Dad. Sue has offered me half the business and the chance to have what I always wanted." He gingerly sat in one of the chairs across from his dad. When he was growing up, they had only been used when company came over.

"Really? You always talked about having a shop of your own." His dad narrowed his gaze, as if about to make some point, then shrugged instead.

Vin was going to ask him what he wanted to say, but the doorbell rang, and Vin answered it. "Hey, Jane, come on in." Oscar got excited, and Vin lifted him into his arms to calm him and keep Oscar from jumping all over her. "I hear you have an offer for the shop."

"Of a sort," she answered. His dad joined them, shook her hand, and then they all sat at the dining room table. "The offer is more for the property than the shop." She passed the paperwork over. The amount seemed fair enough. "They are only interested in the land itself. I believe their plan is to tear down the shop and the greenhouse and build two homes on the property."

Vin felt his stomach fall through the floor. "They only want the land."

Jane nodded. "That's what I understand. It's an all-cash offer, so there are no contingencies regarding financing." Even she seemed disappointed as she went over the details, which seemed to check all of the boxes except for the fact that the shop and greenhouse would be gone. The next time Vin came home, there would be houses where his mother and father had worked all those years.

Vin excused himself and went to the kitchen to get a drink of water. He looked out the window at the backyard and the greenhouse beyond it. The glass of the greenhouse sparkled in the sun now that it had been cleaned. Vin remembered playing in the yard when he was a kid and pretending the greenhouse was a glittering city under a dome.

"What do you want to do?" Jane asked.

"Let me think about it and I'll get back to you in a few days. Is that okay?" his dad asked, and he heard Jane agree. They talked for a few minutes while Vin grew cold. People said goodbye to their pasts all the time, and yet this seemed changed somehow. He'd gone to California to find something different, but he'd always known that his mom and dad would be here for him. Now his mom was gone, and the thought of someone tearing down the shop and greenhouse made him feel as if he was losing her all over again. It was a stupid notion, and one he knew he should just let it go. His dad was moving on, and he needed to do the same thing.

Vin finished his glass of water and put it in the sink before joining the two of them at the table. "I'll talk to you soon. The offer is good for two days, so take your time," Jane said, leaving the paperwork. "If either of you has any questions, please give me a call." She shook hands with both of them. Then Vin showed her to the door and thanked her for coming over.

"What are you going to do?" Vin asked once he joined his dad at the table.

His dad shrugged. "I don't think I have a choice." He pushed the chair back and got up and wandered out of the room. "That place was our lives. Your mother and I built it together and ran it as a team." Vin followed the sound of his voice to where his dad stood at the sliding doors looking out the back of the family room. "But things change, and I can't hold on to a past that isn't coming back. So I guess I'll sell it, then make sure I'm not here when the bulldozers come." He turned and sat on the sofa, Oscar jumping right up to provide comfort.

What the hell did that mean?

UPSTAIRS IN his room, he closed the door and dialed LA. "Vin, it's good to hear from you." Sue was all energy and excitement. "Everything is going great. Will you be back on Monday? I could sure use some of your design expertise."

"What has you so stoked?" Vin asked. After the last call, she'd seemed as if she was on her last nerve.

"The buyers had a change of heart. I think they expected me to just roll over when they walked away. I signed the paperwork for the buyout yesterday, and they'll take over the shop in forty-five days." There was plenty of noise behind her, and Vin waited. The background sound cut off, and Vin knew she was in her tiny office. "I made sure that they knew how valuable you are to the business, and they want to keep you on. I expect that they'll want to talk to you when you get back about position and salary and all that."

"Who is the buyer?" Vin asked, his suspicions rising right along with his disappointment. His chance at part ownership had just flown out the window.

"Mason's Flowers," she answered, and the chill at the base of his gut grew and became frigid. Mason's was a large company and had a stable of designers that put together arrangements that were sold through their stores and website. Almost everything was corporate. "Now before you start to worry, I raved about you and told them how much I depended on you. They were talking about making you the store manager." She said it with such gusto, but Vin could only bring himself to shrug. "Like I said, when you get back, they'll want to sit down and talk with you. They'd be a fool to let you go, and we both know it." She seemed to settle down. "I know that isn't why you called. Is there something I can do for you?"

Vin had intended to tell her about what was going on here and ask for her thoughts, but that seemed ridiculous now. "No. I guess not. Thanks for telling me. It sounds like there will be a lot of interesting changes happening soon." He put his best face on the situation, then hung up and went back downstairs. His dad was making dinner, but Vin wasn't hungry, so he slipped out the sliding glass doors, making sure Oscar stayed inside.

He wandered across the yard and unlocked the shop, went inside, and closed the door. He went right over to the worktable and stood behind it the way his mother had, hands on the worn wooden top. "I don't know what to do, Mom," he said out loud. Vin missed her, and this seemed like the place where her spirit remained. "Things aren't working out the way I'd hoped they would. Dad wants me to reopen this place and run it for him. But I don't want to do that. I desperately want to have a place of my own, one that can *be* my own. I thought that was what I was getting, at least partly, in LA, but that's not going to happen now." He listened for his mother's advice, but of course she didn't answer or offer any wisdom.

The door to the shop opened, and Vin jumped half a mile as his dad came inside with Oscar prancing at the end of his leash. "You scared me." He put his hand over his heart, trying to breathe it back into a normal speed.

"I didn't mean to," his dad said as he closed the door. "Look, son, I sort of heard you."

"Nothing wrong with your ears, is there?" Vin groused.

His father snorted. "Everything else is going to hell, but not my ears. They're as sharp as they ever were. And you weren't exactly quiet." He let Oscar off the leash, and the dog began exploring. "This is where I come to talk to your mother too." He sighed.

"She was always happiest when she was standing right where you are."

"Yeah, I know. And Dad, I know what you want me to do. But I can't run this for you. I can't be Mom," he added.

His dad crossed the room and stood across the table from him. "Son, I don't want you to be. For one thing, no one could ever replace your mother. But I think you misunderstood our earlier conversation. I don't want you to run this for me. I'm giving it to you to run for yourself. Do what you want. Bring it back to life, and I'll be with you the whole way. You have to know what." There were tears in his father's eyes.

"But what about the offer?" Vin asked, and his dad shrugged.

"What about it? If you want to create your own Eden here, then I say screw the money and do it. Take your designs and set up the greenhouse as a showplace if you want. Bring all those ideas of yours to life. I have tons of retired friends who can make anything. Then you can rent them out for parties and weddings, if that's what you want. But whatever you decide, do it because it feels right to you."

Vin leaned against the table, because suddenly his legs felt like jelly. "But what if it doesn't work?"

His father's eyes widened. "Is this about fear? Are you afraid it won't work out? Is that what had you stepping back from Casey too?" He shook his head. "A coward dies a thousand deaths, the brave man only once."

"Yeah, I know, Dad, but—"

"Fuck it," his dad said, and Vin nearly laughed. That was so out of character. "Fuck the fear that's holding you back. Fuck it all. You can have anything you want in life. You just have to have the guts to go after it." He gripped Vin's shoulder. "That means in life, in love… all of it. Don't be afraid to go for what you want. I did."

"And what did you get?" Vin asked.

His dad smiled. "Your mother. It was the best decision I ever made." He let his hands fall to his side. "You know what your mother always said about important decisions…."

"Sleep on them," they said together, and for the first time in days, Vin felt like things just might be going in the right direction.

CHAPTER 10

"Daddy, are you okay?" Brianna asked, coming into his bedroom. "Did you and Mr. Vin have a fight? If you did, you should say sorry and then kiss and make up." She giggled while burying her face in the extra pillow. "I saw you kissing." When she stopped giggling, she sat up and gave him a peck on the cheek.

"Mr. Vin and I just want different things. We didn't really fight or anything." How did he explain that the thought of someone else leaving could hurt so deeply? When Alicia had left years ago, it had hurt. But nothing near as badly as the thought of Vin doing the same thing. Maybe it was best for his own heart and for Brianna if he just put some distance between them. "And it's okay."

"But I like Mr. Vin. He's nice, and he listens to me." Tags jingled, and Winston jumped up on the bed. Brianna slid closer to him, growing quiet. "Why did Mommy try to take me away?"

Sometimes she could change gears so fast. "I don't know. I think maybe she's angry with me." That was the simplest answer he had, and there was no way he wanted Brianna to feel guilty. Alicia had made it through surgery and was going to be okay. At least he hadn't had to have a worse conversation with his daughter.

"But I saw Mr. Vin and you chasing us, trying to get me back." She burrowed closer, and Casey held her tight.

"Yes. I wanted you back more than anything in the world." He kissed the top of her head. "I'll always want you, and I'll always… always… always want you to be safe and happy."

"Is that why you and Mr. Vin got me Winston?" she asked. "I love him, Daddy."

"I know you do, and I love you." He hugged her.

She hugged him and sat still, a quiet moment that he'd treasure forever. "Daddy, did you want to marry Mr. Vin?" Brianna asked. "You love him, right? Because you kissed him." Sometimes she had a way of coming back to the one thing he didn't want to talk about, no matter how hard he might try to change the subject.

"It isn't that simple sometimes." God, he wished it was. There were so many times when he wished that real life fit Brianna's notions. She was so kind and saw things in such simple, clear terms. "We should go let Winston out so he can go potty. Then we need to feed him and make breakfast." She hurried out of the room with Winston right behind her. Casey took the time to get dressed and washed up. He hurried down the stairs, then called Winston and let him out in the fenced yard, making sure the gate was closed, where he did his business and ran around for a while, chasing butterflies and anything else that caught his attention. Then Casey filled his bowl and set it down, making sure he had fresh water.

"Daddy, I was supposed to do it," Brianna scolded.

Casey put the food back so she could measure it out. "Call Winston to come in."

He smiled as she hurried to the backyard and pulled open the door with the hand that wasn't in a pink sling. "Winston!" she called at the top of her lungs.

"Sweetheart, he hears a lot better than you do. There's no need to yell," Casey told her as the dog bounded inside and attacked his bowl. The food vanished as though vacuumed up; then Winston settled down under the kitchen table. When Brianna left the room, the dog followed her to the living room, where he jumped up on the sofa, peering out the front window, tail wagging. He barked once and then jumped down again before heading to the front door just before the bell rang.

"Daddy, it's Mr. Vin," Brianna said.

"How's your arm?" Vin's voice traveled through the house and settled right in Casey's gut whether he wanted it to or not. "I love the sling. Pink is definitely your color."

"Thank you," Brianna said, sounding so grown-up. Casey wiped his hands and went to the door to find out what was going on.

"Hey, Casey," Vin said softly as he stood back up. Brianna hurried off, and Vin closed the door behind him. "I take it Brianna loves Winston." He seemed nervous, and his gaze tilted more toward the floor.

"She does." Casey swallowed. "Oh, and I got clearance to go back to work on Monday. I was also notified that Renaldo and Alicia have been denied bail for fear they'll leave the country. So it seems that most things are going to work out. According to the chief, Alicia's sticking to her story that she had no idea what Renaldo was doing but had glommed onto him because she thought he could help her get custody of Brianna. We believe that Renaldo was importing contraband drugs—that's his family business." Casey shook his head. "He's out of business now, though, and that little black notebook held so much information that the department is having a blast rounding up the rest of his associates. What happened at the greenhouse was only part of it. But it's over now. And Brianna is safe." The relief that washed over him was indescribable.

"Why did he try to take Brianna? That seems like a huge blunder on his part."

"Alicia thinks it was for her, and Renaldo isn't talking, but I suspect he wanted her for leverage." Casey blew out a deep breath to calm his racing heart. How close he came to losing her….

Vin nodded slowly. "Look, I came to tell you that I'm sorry. I…." He sighed. "Dad got an offer on the shop, but they just wanted the land, and they were going to tear down everything else. Sue sold her shop after all, and…. Crap, I'm doing this all wrong." He wiped his forehead with the back of his hand.

"Are you going back anyway?" Casey asked.

"Yes. I have to go back as planned because I need to give my notice and arrange to sell stuff before I come back here. I was scared, and, well, I was thinking some things that aren't true. Dad has decided to give me the shop and greenhouse, and I'm going to figure out how to reopen it but make it my own." He came closer. "I know I was a fool."

The disbelief must have shown in Casey's expression. "Is the fact that Sue changed her mind the only reason you're staying?"

"Honestly, that's a part of it. But I think it only helped me realize what was really important. Dad looked me in the eyes last night and told me I was just acting chickenshit about the whole thing, and he was right there too. The shop in Los Angeles was a sure thing, and I would have had an experienced partner. Here, I'm on my own and working without a net, both with the store and with you, and…." He snapped his mouth shut. "Now I'm rambling like an idiot."

Casey shook his head.

"I'm not rambling?" Vin asked.

Casey grinned. "Oh, you're rambling, and yeah, you were kind of an idiot, but maybe so was I, for expecting you to stay here after less than a week together. I wanted me to be enough of a reason for you to stay. But I guess…."

"You should be enough, and you are. But I'm not staying for you, though I want that chance. That's all I'm asking for. I'm staying and I'm going to build a business here because I want to. Like you told me before… I'm going to do it for me. But I'm hoping you'll be there too, because I can't do this alone." He bit his lower lip and shifted his weight from foot to foot. "I'm going to stay with Dad once I get back from LA, and, well…."

Casey smiled, and Vin immediately echoed it. "What is it you want from me?" It seemed strange to ask that, but Casey needed to know where he stood. The whirlwind that had been his emotions over the past week needed to come to a stop. "I need to know what you feel and what you're thinking. Do you see this as a convenient fling that you had while you were on vacation? Because I have to think of more than just me. There's Brianna, and…."

Vin dove closer, cupped Casey's cheeks in his hands, and pressed their lips together in a kiss that threatened to stop the world from spinning. Casey was so shocked that he held his arms at his sides for maybe a full minute before closing them around Vin and pulling him tight to his chest. "What I want is you," Vin whispered, his words rough and his eyes wide, with fire glowing behind them. "I have ever since we were both in high school. So I'm going to have to leave for a while, but I will be back as soon as I can settle things."

"And what about your life there? Is it going to pull at you?" Casey tried not to be nervous, but he couldn't help it. "And what if Sue finds out you're leaving and makes you a better offer, or…."

Vin shook his head. "I thought she was my friend as well as my boss. But she's just out for herself. My eyes have been opened to a lot of things—about myself, my dad, and most importantly, what it is that I really want." Vin paused, resting their foreheads together. "I guess the real question is, what do you want? What is going to make you deliriously happy?"

Casey made a show of thinking about it. Then he kissed Vin again.

"Daddy, did you say you were sorry?" Brianna asked from behind him. In all his excitement about Vin, he had forgotten about Brianna for a few seconds, and of course she had wandered in. "Mr. Vin, are you going to marry Daddy because you kissed him?"

Casey did his best to keep from chuckling while Vin met his gaze, his eyes filled with questions. "Maybe someday. Your daddy and I are figuring things out. Is that okay?"

"Then are you going to take care of Daddy from now on?" she asked.

"Yes, I promise I will," Vin answered her with a bright, warm smile. Casey really liked the thought of that, and he'd look after Vin right back.

Brianna nodded seriously, and Casey waited for her next question. But it seemed she had all the information she needed and simply wandered over to play with her dolls while Winston curled up in one of the chairs to watch.

"Well, that was anticlimactic, wasn't it?" Vin asked. "I was expecting more of a grilling from Brianna."

"Oh, we'll get it. Just not now." Casey stifled a yawn because he'd been up most of the night. When his phone rang, Brianna ran for it.

"Hi, Grandma," Brianna said brightly. "Guess what? I got a dog! His name is Winston, and he's really nice. You're going to like him. Oh, and Mr. Vin is going to stay, and he and Daddy were kissing." She shuddered dramatically as only a little girl can. "I'm not gonna kiss boys… ever." She made a face, and Vin broke out laughing.

"Let me talk to her," Casey said, and Brianna gave him the phone.

"Well, I guess a lot has happened in a day. I was calling because I wanted to check on my granddaughter, but it seems she's fine. Which surprises me."

"Me too," he said softly. "But I'm going to go ahead and find someone she can talk with about it. I'm sure there are going to be issues, and we need to know how to handle them. She's asked a few questions so far, and I've answered them as best I can." He felt a little underwater over all that, but he'd do whatever Brianna needed.

"Good. I'm downtown having coffee. Maybe Brianna and this dog of hers could come over later." She seemed happy. "It would give you and Vin a chance to really talk things through. Brianna needs stable people in her life. Make sure he's really going to be there, because I will come after him if he hurts either one of you." Sometimes Casey's mother could be frightening, and this was one of those times. But she meant well, and Casey reminded himself of that.

"Yes. I'll get Brianna ready."

"Good. She and I can go shopping for things for the dog so we'll have them when they come to my house," she added, and Casey thanked her before ending the call.

Casey had honestly thought she'd fight him on the dog. His mother had changed, and maybe this change had staying power.

"Let's go make some breakfast," Casey said, taking Vin's hand.

"SO WHAT are you going to do with the shop and greenhouse now that you have it?" Casey asked that afternoon. He'd left Brianna with his mother and had joined Vin in the shop.

"I don't know," he said as he wandered around. "I need to change some things. This place, the room itself, is all my mother. And I loved her, but that isn't what I want." He closed his eyes and stood still. "I keep hoping for a vision to come to me, but all I keep seeing are things the way my mother had them."

"Then start with paint. Change the color of the shop. Make it the one you want." Casey looked down. "Your mother painted the floor, but there's planked oak under that. We could sand it down, then finish it with a high-traffic varnish like they use on gym floors. And as for your mother's worktable…." He turned to Vin. "You could use it as a display. It has all that character and would be wonderful that way."

Vin bounded over and threw his arms around him. "That's perfect," he said, grinning from ear to ear. "I can repurpose some of Mom's things in the decorating, but still make them mine." Vin kissed him quickly and then did it again, passion rising within seconds. Vin wound his legs around Casey's waist, and Casey supported him under his tight butt and took him to the worktable. He wanted Vin now, and the thought of waiting an hour longer drove him crazy. Vin was staying, and Casey needed to make him his.

His hands shook as he fumbled with his belt, getting it open and Vin's as well. "Do you really want to do this here?" Vin breathed.

Casey nodded. "You said you wanted to make this yours…." He stepped back, tugged off Vin's pants, and dropped them to the side before attacking his lips once again. He was too far gone to think, much less work the damned buttons of Vin's shirt. But once that fabric parted and all of Vin was bared to him, he growled, his hands taking in every plane and curve of the man he loved. He raked over him with his eyes and fingers, inhaling the building scent of desire. He managed to get his own clothes off before he bent over Vin, taking all of him in, touching him in as many places as possible.

"Yes…," Vin breathed, and Casey groaned, wishing he had brought some protection. "Tested?"

"Last month for the job. You?" Casey was shocked that his lips were still able to do anything but take possession of Vin's.

"Six months. No one since," Vin whispered, wrapping his arms around Casey's neck and drawing him closer. "I want you, Casey. I have for the longest time." He pulled Casey into a kiss, and slowly Casey positioned himself and pressed forward. Vin hissed, and Casey stopped. The last thing Casey wanted to do was hurt Vin. Maybe they should have waited…. But Vin pressed against him, holding tighter, and he inched farther inside.

"Oh God," Casey groaned, and Vin whimpered and arched his back until he'd taken all of him.

The physical connection with Vin was incredible, but the emotional message coming through those expressive eyes of his was mind-blowing. He didn't dare turn away and risk losing the connection. The wonder and passion that shone in Vin's eyes were almost more than Casey could take. He had seen things he wished he could forget, but this moment was one he'd remember for the rest of his life. Casey filed the image deep inside, storing it in his heart. As he began to move, Vin's eyes widened and his mouth hung open. Casey snapped another shot in his mind's eye, storing image after image, sound and scent, even the way the breeze blew around the building, as though it, too, wanted to be part of their coupling. A serenade.

"Am I hurting you?" he asked.

"No," Vin whimpered, drawing their lips together. "Just don't stop." He breathed deeply, holding Casey tightly as the table rocked right along with them. Casey began to wonder if the damned thing was going to last, but stopping was out of the question. He was way too far gone. He rocked faster, and Vin's cries grew louder until he stiffened and drew Casey tight, pulling Casey close to the edge until, in a heartbeat, they both tumbled over together.

Vin held still, and Casey didn't dare move until their bodies separated. Thankful for some paper towels, he gently wiped Vin's luminous skin. "You know, there are some definite advantages to making love in a bed. I get to hold you afterward, and…."

"There are no splinters in my butt," Vin quipped, slowly bringing himself to his feet. He sighed and once again looked through the shop space. "Well, one thing is for sure." He reached for his clothes and began pulling them on, tossing Casey's to him.

"What's that?" Casey asked.

Vin's shirt hung open, and his pants barely clung to his hips as he closed the distance between them. "I'm damned lucky to have gotten a second chance with you… with everything." He slipped his arms around Casey's neck and drew him into a kiss as intense as any they'd shared.

"Me too. Sometimes we get a second chance at what really matters," Casey said.

Vin rested his head on Casey's shoulder, and Casey carded his fingers through Vin's soft hair. "At least after that, I'm not going to have to worry about how I'll make this place my own." His mother's worktable, the one they'd just made love on, crashed to the floor as two of the legs gave out. "I know I'll never be able to think of this space the same way again," Vin said.

That was true. Casey would always remember making love to the man who'd held part of his heart for years and now was back in his arms, where he'd stay… a part of his heart, his soul, and his family. What more could he ever want?

EPILOGUE

IT WAS the first day of November—the date that had been circled on his calendar for three months now. It had taken longer than he'd expected to wrap things up in Los Angeles and move back to Carlisle, but he'd done it. Sue had been hurt and angry at first, especially since it seemed the shop buyers had been hoping to acquire his talents along with the shop. Still, he'd given his notice as soon as the sale had gone through, and he'd already cleared out many of his things and arranged for the shipment of others, including all of his designs. He'd long ago been sure to include in his employment agreement that all of his designs were his property—something Sue had forgotten about.

"The greenhouse looks amazing," Casey said as they walked through it. Vin had redesigned it, re-working parts and adding on a section. A fountain now gurgled in the center, surrounded by poinsettias. Lush plants of all varieties filled the rest of the greenhouse. It looked like an arboretum, except everything was for sale and ready to be taken home. "And the glass… I thought you were crazy to replace it all, but I get it now." He looked upward, entranced with the view of the early evening sky, dark against the shimmer of lights overhead.

"It holds in the heat better," Vin said. "I can keep this going all winter without it costing a fortune." Groundwater flowed throughout the greenhouse within a series of pipes, pumped from a well, then circulated back. It was a constant temperature, and through the magic of heat transfer, it, along with the sun, kept the greenhouse warm using minimal energy.

"Mr. Vin!" Brianna hurried up with Winston on a leash. "It's so pretty." She lifted her gaze upward. "Are they floating?" she asked, staring at his hanging arrangements. The filaments had to catch the light just right in order to be seen. He'd also had some of his other designs recreated, including his imposing candelabra. They stood at the far end of the greenhouse, drawing the eye down. Just from the pictures on the website, he'd already rented them for six weddings. And he'd created a Robins Floral website showcasing his original designs, and the orders were coming in, fast and furious.

"When do we open?" Brianna asked. She had been designated as the official greeter to welcome people as they came in.

"Half an hour," Vin told her with a smile. "You might want to take Winston back to the house so he and Oscar can play. There'll be a lot of people here, and he might get scared."

When she hurried toward the door, Casey called to her, "Put your coat on before you go out!"

"I will." Then she was out the door, leaving the two of them alone.

"How did things go with Alicia's court date?" Vin asked, not wanting to bring it up in front of Brianna. The two of them had agreed that Casey would figure out how to explain what was happening with her mother when the time was right. But her specter was completely absent today—both in reality and in spirit.

Casey had been doing a lot of soul-searching lately, mainly about his job. Now that Vin was making his dream come true, it had made Casey look at his own. Casey had told him that he'd joined the force because it was something his family had expected him to do. But was it his dream?

Vin has seen Casey come to love his job and really seemed to like being part of a team. He had great colleagues, a boss who stood behind him, and friends that felt more like part of the family. Was that Casey's original dream? No. But then, it had turned into something even better. And Vin was glad Casey was happy now.

The sound of a throat clearing had Vin turning toward the shop door. "What is it, Dad?"

He held up the box that Vin had found in the basement months ago. Vin nodded, and they all headed toward the shop, which looked like a winter wonderland, complete with twinkling lights and all the flowers of the season.

"Where's Brianna?" Casey asked.

"Inside with your mother," Vin's father answered. "She's on puppy duty this evening but said she'd send Brianna out just before opening time." He set the box on a newly finished wooden countertop and removed the tape from the four sides. A few months ago, Casey had managed to pick the lock, but rather than open it, they'd then sealed the box until tonight. It was their way of including her.

"Open it, Vin," his dad said, and Vin lifted the lid. He didn't know what he expected to find inside. Maybe his mom had left something as mundane as money, or maybe a note for him or his dad. But that wasn't what was inside. Instead, Vin lifted out a bunch of cards.

"I remember these," Vin said, gently touching the construction paper creations he'd made in grade school. Mother's Day, Christmas, birthdays—they were all there. He set them gently on the counter until he got to a few more commercial ones.

"There's a note," Casey said, and Vin pulled it out and unfolded it to reveal his mother's familiar handwriting. His chest grew warm at the sight, and he smiled.

Vin,

A mother has dreams, but it's never a good thing for a parent to push theirs on their children. You have

*to go out in the world and find your place in it. More
than anything, I want you to be happy. I always have.*

*My greatest dream was opening the greenhouse.
It was what I always wanted, and your father and I
worked together for years to build the business and
make it something we could both be proud of. I always hoped to be able to pass the shop on to you. I
know, a parent's dreams are not always the same as
her child's. But it's my dream, and I can make it what
I'd like.*

Vin smiled as his mother's voice echoed in his
head. He could almost see her sitting at her worktable, writing this during a quiet moment.

*Regardless of how things turn out and where
your path takes you, I want you to know that I'm
proud of you and I always will be.*

Just be happy. That's all I ever wanted.

Mom

Vin sighed and was glad he hadn't read the note
out loud. He would never have made it through without his voice breaking. He showed the note to his
father and Casey before placing it back in the box
along with the other things and closing the lid. He
moved a few things around on the shelf on the north
wall, placing the box on it under his favorite picture
of his mother smiling from behind her worktable.

"Daddy, Mr. Vin!" Brianna said as she came
inside, closing the door quickly. "There are lots of
people outside, including Mr. Les and Mr. Dex from
the bookstore and Mr. Carter and Mr. Red." She was
so excited. Mack took his place behind the counter,
and Vin took Casey's hand and squeezed it tightly.

"Are you ready?" he asked Brianna, and she grinned.

Vin met Casey's gaze and reached for the door, but Casey stopped him. "I'm not sure how you wish someone good luck on a flower-shop opening, so will this do?" Casey kissed him and then stepped back. Vin opened the door.

"Welcome to Robins Flowers, where each bouquet is made with love." He couldn't help glancing at the picture of his mother, then smiling at Casey, as the first customer came through the doors.

Keep reading for an excerpt from
New Leaf
by Andrew Grey

AFTER HOURS of talking and listening, Dex was worn out, and the time change was getting to him. Fortunately, he found Jane.

"Go for a walk. This will go on until the funeral. Your mother was loved, but it's going to be overwhelming if you don't take a break." She smiled. "Take the keys to the store if you want."

Dex gratefully went out the back door and through the yard, weaving along the back alley to the store. Then, after unlocking the rear door, he let himself inside.

The familiar scent of dust, books, and his mother nearly sent him reeling. This he remembered. Dex closed the door and turned on the lights as he wandered through the small back room with its boxes and shelves. His mother didn't keep much back here. She never had. She'd always said that she couldn't sell what was back here, so she kept as much of her stock out front as possible. Dex perused the area, remembering the corner where she'd set up a table and chairs. He had sat there for hours doing his homework, coloring, crafts—all of it in his own corner of the store. Oh, the hours he'd spent in this space with his mom. She always came back to check on him, and if there was no one in the store, she'd read to him or they'd color together until the bell on the front door jangled. It got to the point that he hated that bell because it meant she'd have to go back to work.

He peeked into some of the boxes before stepping through the curtain and out behind the register. The lights were off, but the sun shone in through the front windows. Everything looked as though his mother would return at any moment to open up. The shelves were all in order, and even the notebook she kept on the counter behind the register sat in its usual spot, surrounded by the trinkets and bookmark display. Dex lifted the counter and lowered it again once he'd stepped out from behind it, then wandered the aisles, looking over the rack of children's books. His mother had read most of them to him at one point. Of course, there were newer ones as well, but he continued on, checking over the shelves.

More books were turned cover forward to fill the shelves than he remembered. When he was a kid, the store had always been packed. But now it seemed staged—behind the single titles, there was nothing.

The inventory he remembered his mother carrying wasn't in the store. Maybe it was just the children's section?

He continued to the adult areas of the store. There he found only a few hardcover books, and of the titles she had, his mother only had two or three copies. Dex knew independent bookstores had been having a difficult time in the past years because of Amazon, but every time he had asked his mother how the store was, she had told him it was fine. Maybe things hadn't been as rosy as his mother projected.

A knock on the front door startled him. He went up front, turned the lock, and opened the door. "Can I help you? We're closed for the next few days."

"I'm sorry. I was just passing, and I always stop by when I'm downtown." The man lifted his gaze, and Dex was struck by the most intensely blue eyes he had ever seen.

"My mother passed away and…." Damn, it was hard just to say the words. "The store will be closed until after the funeral." He put his hand over his mouth, willing himself not to fall apart. He had been okay a few minutes ago, but the grief was suddenly too much to bear.

"I'm so sorry. She was a nice lady." He paused, lowering his gaze slightly, looking like he might leave. "You're Sarah's son? She talked a lot about you. She said you were going to be in the movies." He smiled.

Dex swallowed hard. His mind skipped to how hunkalicious this guy was, with his hair all askew and his wrinkled shirt open just enough to allow Dex to catch a glimpse of a smattering of brown chest hair.

"Yes. I'm Dex." It was nice that his mom had talked about him. Even if he hadn't had any real success in Hollywood, his mother had always been proud of him anyway, he thought, his heart hitching.

"I was a regular customer of your mom's. I try to support local businesses, and she'd order in the books I wanted. That way she got the business instead of the big online places." He smiled, and Dex nodded.

"Did she have an order for you?" He wondered where his mother might have put it if she had.

"No. There were a few books I wanted, though. Still, I can come back once you're open again…." He leaned closer. "You are opening again, aren't you?" The blue in his eyes grew darker. "This is the only place in town that would order books for me. At least, the ones I wanted." He looked up and down the street. "I've got a weakness for romance—the masculine kind."

"I see…."

He put his hand over his mouth. "Of course. Sarah told me she had a gay son." He cleared his throat. "I'm sorry. I'm Les. Les Gable." He shook his hand. "I'm sorry to keep you. I'll come back later." He paused. "I just want to tell you that your mom was the greatest. She cared so much about everyone. I'm going to miss her." Then he turned and, with a wave, hurried down the sidewalk.

Dex closed the door and locked it again. It seemed his mother had had an impact on a lot of people in town. She had always loved books and got a great deal of joy from reading, something she had passed on to Dex.

He walked through the store before returning to the back room. He found the safe where his mother always kept it, and searched his memory for the combination. She had told him what it was years ago, and luckily the numbers returned to him. He opened it and peered inside, where he found less than a hundred dollars, her starting bank for the day. He also pulled out the store accounts book. Then he closed the safe door and locked it again.

He wasn't sure what else he wanted to do, but he didn't want to go back to the house. The grief gathering was probably still going on, and he'd had enough. His mother was gone, and Dex needed to try to process the loss alone. He didn't need dozens of people talking about his mother for him to know her. His mom was here in this building—in each book, as well as in the way she'd painted each wall a different color because she thought it would be cheerful. The only problem was that she'd picked the brightest colors possible. Dex was afraid his eyes would start bleeding if he didn't do something about it soon. Especially that grass-green carpeting. "Mom, I love you, but your decorating was a nightmare," he said out loud, smiling. That was his mother. She loved what she loved, and to hell with what everyone else thought.

Dex set down the books and headed for the bathroom, gasping when he opened the door. Apparently where the bathroom in the house was Whoville, the one in the store was all Alice in Wonderland, and it had gotten the same treatment, including a Mad

Hatter toilet-paper holder and a Queen of Hearts toilet cozy. The White Rabbit bounded over one of the walls, but it was Alice being sucked down the rabbit hole that made him laugh. It came with a reminder to flush. This was his mother in a nutshell. She could be out there, and yet she could also be so clever.

He shut the door, unable to use the bathroom, and retrieved the record book. It was time to go back to the house. At least now he could review his mom's records and figure out if it was viable to keep the store going.

He had a task to accomplish, something that would fill some hours and keep him from moping around. If the store was his mother's legacy, Dex needed to see if there was a way to move forward. He pulled open the rear door and locked it behind him, then headed back toward the house.

He decided to take a roundabout route, walking down to the square as the clock in the old courthouse chimed the hour. He paused and smiled. He remembered being in the store, listening for that bell, because most days, when it chimed six times, his mom would close up and they would go home. He shook his head as if to clear the memories. Something around every corner seemed to remind him of her. The trees had all leafed out, shading the streets. Dex wiped his eyes. In his mind's eye, he could see his mom and dad in their backyard, music drifting out from the house as they danced to a cascade of flower petals.

At the time, he'd considered it horribly embarrassing, especially when his mother had backed away from his dad insisting that she teach Dex to dance. Dex had fought it with everything he had. He hadn't wanted to learn to dance. But she'd made him. Damn, what he wouldn't give to dance with her with one last time.

"Dex?"

He turned and once again met Les's blue eyes. His heart beat a little faster and his throat dried in an instant, especially seeing the heat and interest in those eyes. Dex was used to people looking at him with hunger, but this was something more. "I just left the library and was on my way back to my apartment. What are you up to?"

"I finished up in the store and figured it was time to go home." He nodded in the direction he was going, and Les fell into step along with him, walking slowly. Dex realized that his one leg seemed stiff. He shortened his usual stride so Les wouldn't have to strain to keep up.

Les smiled at him. "Sarah always told me stories about you when I was in the store. She said that you're an actor working in LA."

"I haven't been working all that much lately, unfortunately. Unless you count porn," Dex said, his voice deadpan.

Les stopped midstride. "You did porn?"

Dex shook his head, grinning. "Oh God, no. My last audition was supposed to be a serious role, but well, it didn't turn out that way. My mother was always supportive, but I can't help but think her support would not stretch to cover that." He chuckled. "Though maybe Mom would have just told me to do my best, then rented a copy later so she could tell me what I'd done wrong." He chuckled. "I would have to say that the most embarrassing thing I can think of is my mother going out to get a copy of Shaving Ryan's Privates or something, so she could rate my performance."

Les chuckled. "It must have been nice to have that kind of support in your life. I never did. My family wasn't anywhere near as open-minded as your mom, that's for sure. My folks were very predictable. 'You will go to college, you will go to church, you will not be gay or have gay thoughts.'" The humor left his voice and his posture became more rigid when he spoke of his parents.

Dex had always known he'd been lucky, especially when it came to his mom, but he sometimes forgot how fortunate. "I never knew how Mom was going to take anything. You remember what it was like to be a teenager and all you wanted to do was shock your parents? I'd do that, and Mom would look at me and say, 'It's okay, I support you and will always love you.' Then the next day she'd decide that the upstairs bathroom needed painting and I'd walk in and get a surprise of my own when the walls were jet black… or neon yellow. The hall bathroom upstairs has been both at one time. I think it was her way of shocking me right back. And her offbeat decorating skills usually did the trick."

Les laughed out loud, his stance loosening. "She would do the funniest things. One time when I came into the store, she had the shelves pulled back from one of the walls and was painting it Barbie pink, just so she could see how it would look."

"That's my mom," Dex agreed.

"At least she liked color. My mother painted the entire house this off-white color. She called it Palest Peony or something, and every wall in every room was the same color, all through the house. I had to beg her to let me do my room in blue. She eventually let me, but only if I promised that if it didn't work out, I'd paint it back. The furniture was every shade of brown, and the carpet beige. It was like living in a forest in permanent winter. Mom's idea of adding color was bringing in black accents… because they went with everything." Les began to laugh. "My dad hated it. So for Christmas, he used to get her really bright knick-knacks. They would be on display for a while and then suddenly they'd disappear." He smiled.

"You're kidding, right?" Dex asked. When Les shook his head, Dex added, "You should see the guest bedroom upstairs. It has this psychedelic wall-paper, as if the person who created it had done acid back in the sixties. I have no idea where Mom found it, but I'm surprised anyone who's stayed over hasn't suffered from seizures." He paused. "You know, that could be why Mom didn't get many guests. They'd stay one night and detour to the hospital on their way out of town."

Les shrugged, smiling. "You know what they say—after three days, both fish and guests begin to stink. Maybe it was her way of controlling the odor." He tilted his head adorably to the side, and Dex took a second to enjoy the view. Les had a strong jaw and an expressive face that pulled Dex in. His high cheek-bones gave him an almost regal look, and yet his eyes danced with mischief. And he had a sense of humor, which was necessary… if just to get through the trials and tribulations of life. Dex had definitely needed one with his mother. She had sometimes been a handful.

"My mom's guest room…."

"Let me guess, slightly pinky off-white," Dex teased.

"Yup. I remember having a friend for a sleepover. I showed him into the room—he set down his bag and fell onto the bed, asleep instantly." He grinned and Dex rolled his eyes before chuckling lightly.

"So your mom was color-challenged. And mine was a color ninja, never afraid of anything." They approached the house, and Dex groaned as a couple went inside carrying a casserole dish. "I swear to God, the house is going to explode with all the grief food people are bringing." He patted his stomach, which did a little roll at the thought. "Want to hazard a guess as to the number of pounds of macaroni and cans of soup that have given their lives already?"

Les shook his head vehemently. "Not on your life." He patted Dex's shoulder, and heat spread through him from the touch. "I need to get home too. But I'll see you later at the store?" His gaze met Dex's, and Dex nodded but made no effort to move away. There was something incredibly attractive about being lost in those eyes, and he was in no hurry to return to reality. Les licked his lips, and just like that, Dex wondered how he tasted. Les was a feast for the eyes, and his musky scent wafted on the breeze. Dex swallowed hard, wishing for more, but there were limits to what he'd do with a guy he'd just met.

It was bad enough that Dex had done things he could never tell his mother in order to try to secure a role. He suppressed a shiver thinking about it. This wasn't Hollywood. Les was just a handsome guy. "I should go inside and make sure Jane isn't overwhelmed."

Les nodded, and Dex shook his hand, then forced himself to turn away from him and walk inside the house.

ANDREW GREY is the author of more than one hundred works of Contemporary Gay Romantic fiction. After twenty-seven years in corporate America, he has now settled down in Central Pennsylvania with his husband of more than twenty-five years, Dominic, and his laptop. An interesting ménage. Andrew grew up in western Michigan with a father who loved to tell stories and a mother who loved to read them. Since then he has lived throughout the country and traveled throughout the world. He is a recipient of the RWA Centennial Award, has a master's degree from the University of Wisconsin–Milwaukee, and now writes full-time. Andrew's hobbies include collecting antiques, gardening, and leaving his dirty dishes anywhere but in the sink (particularly when writing). He considers himself blessed with an accepting family, fantastic friends, and the world's most supportive and loving partner. Andrew currently lives in beautiful, historic Carlisle, Pennsylvania.

Email: andrewgrey@comcast.net
Website:www.andrewgreybooks.com

NEW LEAF
ANDREW GREY

A New Leaf Romance

When Dex Grippon's mother dies, he takes it as a sign—it's time to give up acting and return to his hometown. If he can find a way to save his mother's bookstore, he can preserve the one link he still has to his parents. But keeping an independent bookstore afloat turns out to be more difficult than he anticipated, and Dex isn't the only one who wonders what else his mom might have been selling.

Former cop Les Gable might be off the job, but he has to know what was going on at the bookstore, and he'll do anything to satisfy his curiosity—including befriend the new owner with an offer to help sort out his new business. Something about the bookstore doesn't smell right, and Les is going to find out what.

The problem is that his curiosity about Dex soon far outstrips his interest in what happened at the store. But as curiosity matures into love, the store's past threatens their future. Can Les and Dex untangle the mystery of the bookshop and escape with their relationship—and their lives—intact, or will the whole thing go up in smoke?

www.dreamspinnerpress.com

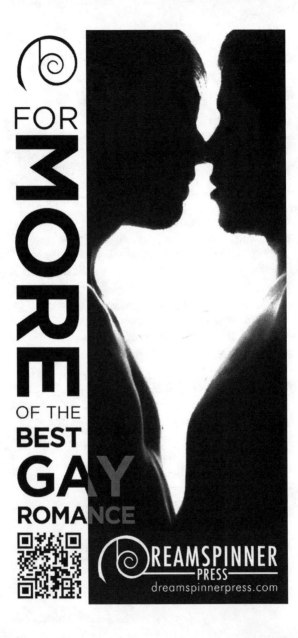